RAEANNE THAYNE

The
Interpreter

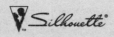
Silhouette®

INTIMATE MOMENTS™

Published by Silhouette Books

America's Publisher of Contemporary Romance

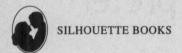

SILHOUETTE BOOKS

RECYCLED PAPER · RECYCLED PAPER

ISBN 0-373-27450-5

THE INTERPRETER

Visit Silhouette Books at www.eHarlequin.com

Printed in Canada.

Books by RaeAnne Thayne

Silhouette Intimate Moments

The Wrangler and the Runaway Mom #960
Saving Grace #995
Renegade Father #1062
*The Valentine Two-Step #1133
*Taming Jesse James #1139
*Cassidy Harte and the Comeback Kid #1144
The Quiet Storm #1218
Freefall #1239
†Nowhere To Hide #1264
†Nothing To Lose #1321
†Never Too Late #1364
The Interpreter #1380

*Outlaw Hartes
†The Searchers

RAEANNE THAYNE

lives in a graceful old Victorian nestled in the rugged mountains of northern Utah, along with her husband and two young children. Her books have won numerous honors, including several readers' choice awards and a RITA® Award nomination by the Romance Writers of America. RaeAnne loves to hear from readers. She can be reached through her Web site at www.raeannethayne.com, or at P.O. Box 6682, North Logan, UT 84341.

To the real Harry Withington and his beautiful wife, Jessie, for opening their home and their hearts to us.

And to Rose Robinson, for all the Tagalog help. Many, many thanks!

Chapter 1

She was in a regular bloody mess.

Bound and gagged in the back of what she thought must be a rented lorry, Jane Withington bit the inside of both cheeks in a vain attempt to keep the panic at bay.

It didn't work. Though she was gnawing hard enough to draw blood, savage fear still prowled in her chest, in her head, through her veins—doing a much better job of choking her than the dirty kerchief they had stuffed in her mouth.

How could she not panic? Any sane woman would, knowing she was on her way to certain death, all because she had never been any kind of a decent poker player.

She wouldn't be in this mess if only she had selected a different Park City restaurant for dinner on her evening off from her duties as an interpreter at the International Trade Summit—if only she hadn't been seated at the booth next to the quartet of men with the low, intense voices, one of whom she recognized, first by his voice and then when she confirmed her suspicions by a furtive look behind her on the pretext of dropping her serviette.

None of this would have happened if she had been able to sneak away without Simon Djami, the Vandelusian trade minister, seeing her—or if she wasn't so damn brilliant with languages and didn't know a word of Vandish, the obscure Southeast Asian dialect they were speaking.

But she *did* know Vandish. And she knew herself well enough to be certain she hadn't been able to hide her shock and horror at what she heard them planning.

"All is in place," one of the Vandish men had said, not even bothering to lower his voice.

"Ah, wonderful," Simon Djami had said. "You have indeed pleased me, my friend. Months of preparation will result in this grand protest, all for the glory of Vandelusia. We will show them the people of Vandelusia are not puppets to be yanked about by godless, unclean western hands."

"It is good you have bought the loyalty of your two FBI lapdogs. With their help we will have the nerve gas canister by Sunday night and will be ready to prepare the detonation device for Wednesday's treaty signing."

Nerve gas? Detonation devices? Good Lord, they were planning a terrorist attack.

The quite pleasant roast duckling she had been enjoying up to that point now congealed in her stomach in a big greasy ball. She had to get out of here, to warn someone!

It was just her bad luck that before she could frantically summon the waitress for her bill so she could escape, Djami walked past her on the way to the men's room. Though she tried to hide behind the book she had brought to keep her company at dinner, she hadn't moved quickly enough.

For one tiny instant, their gazes collided. As she looked into his cold eyes, she saw recognition flicker there—recognition of who she was and exactly what she must have overheard and understood.

She was likely the only person outside of those four men in the entire western United States who spoke Vandish, and in that cold gaze, she saw that her fate had been sealed.

Now, hours later, the lorry hit a deep bump suddenly and Jane gasped as the jarring movement smashed her against unforgiving metal. Her head connected with a crack and for an instant, pain and fear made her woozy. She blinked away the dizziness, then felt warmth trickle down her face. Was she bleeding? She had hit something sharp as she had been jostled against the lorry wall. A screw, perhaps?

She tried to rub her cheek against her shoulder but with her tightly bound hands behind her back, she didn't have the range of motion necessary to staunch the dripping blood.

It seemed the last straw. The fear she had been trying so hard to contain growled and snapped at its leash.

She was utterly helpless in a crisis. Always had been. And this particular crisis was bound to paralyze her. All of this—the gag, the restraints, the awful fear—was too much like *before,* that terrible time she had fiercely tried to wipe from her memory, impossible though that task was.

Just as in her nightmares, she was fifteen again in a foreign country, in the midst of hostile, angry enemies, praying to whoever would listen to her pleas to extricate her. Then, as now, she was a pawn in a game much bigger than she was.

And then, just as now, she had been completely worth-less, unable to focus on anything but the rampaging terror.

Oh, this was horrible. She wanted to curl up into a tight little ball and let the jostling of the lorry rock her to sleep. Dying would be so much less terrifying if she could only sleep through it.

Buck up, darling.

Though she knew it was only her imagination, she could suddenly hear her father's voice in her ear, gruff and hearty and wonderful.

Be strong for me, Janie-girl. You know you're clever enough to get yourself out of this.

She wasn't strong, though, or particularly clever. Harry Withington had always been the brave one, the forceful one in their little family unit of two. She had so wanted to be like him, reckless and brash and bold. Even with the rest of the world exploding around him in chaos, Harry was in-evitably a rock of stability and good sense in a storm-tossed sea. He thrived on those situations that tended to send her spiraling into panic.

Heaven knows, he spent his whole life seeking them out, traveling to all the world's hotspots. She sometimes used to think he much preferred the tumult to the calm.

The thought of her father brought her once more directly to that memory she wanted so desperately to forget. The last time she saw him alive, he had given her much the same advice as he did now in her imagination. *Buck up. Be strong for me. I'll get you out, Janie-girl. You know I will.*

He'd kept that promise as he did all his others—though in the end it had cost him his life, snuffing out all that strength and vitality forever.

She drew in a shuddering breath. She couldn't think of

that now, of her last view of her father while she ran for her life with a squadron of American and British commandos as Harry had been viciously attacked on all sides by her kidnappers.

If she couldn't force that image from her mind, she would never find the courage to escape—and she had to get away, no matter what it took.

She didn't want to die. Not here, not like this.

The lorry rattled across another bump and the door shook on its hinges, separating enough to let in a thin crack of moonlight.

Where were they? she wondered. They had started this journey on highway roads but some time ago her kidnappers had left the relative smoothness of pavement for this jerky, rutted dirt road. The stifling heat inside the lorry had abated somewhat, making her wonder if they had ascended into the coolness of the Utah mountains.

It would make a grim sort of sense. They would want to dispose of her body somewhere remote and isolated where she wouldn't be quickly discovered.

She drew in another sharp breath through the acrid gag. Stop thinking about it and do something!

What, Harry?

Her mind raced as she considered her options. Another drop of blood tickled as it slid down her neck, and the sensation reminded her of the screw that had cut her head. If it was sharp enough to break through flesh, perhaps it could be used to sever the nylon cord securing her arms.

She rose on her knees as best she could, and with her bound hands she searched the general location where she had bumped the inside wall of the lorry. Long moments passed until at last the sharp edge poked the pad of her thumb.

Her heart pumping, Jane dragged her hands across it
again and again. For what felt like hours, she fought the
jostling of the vehicle until she felt the cord begin to fray.
The minor success accelerated her efforts and a few frantic moments later her hands at last slipped free.

Sweet relief washed through her as she ripped away the
gag and quickly worked the knotted cords around her ankles.

Good girl, her father's voice in her head praised.

Now what? She sat back on her heels, considering her
options. The lorry rattled over another bump and the rear
doors jostled open again slightly, spilling that thin slice of
moonlight inside.

Could she push them open from the inside? she wondered. It was worth a try. She had nothing to lose, after all.

She scrambled toward the doors, looking out that narrow window at the world outside. All she could see were
trees—dark forests of evergreens and the spindly, ghostly
trunks of aspens.

There were bound to be wild animals out there. Deer,
elk, badgers. Did they have bears in this part of Utah? she
wondered.

Jane gnawed at her lip. What a lowering reflection on
her psyche that she found that vast, dark wilderness outside almost more terrifying than what inevitably awaited
her at the end of this journey.

No. She was Harry Withington's daughter. She couldn't
just cower and let these men kill her to hide their evil plans.
For once in her cowardly life, she would force herself to
draw on whatever tiny portion of courage and strength her
father had passed on to her.

She knew nothing about cargo lorry doors but she had
to assume these either weren't bolted properly or the bolt

had loosened from the rutted road, otherwise she likely wouldn't be seeing this moonlight. At the next bump when the doors separated slightly, she threw all her weight against them. They quivered but held fast.

Come on, she prayed. To her everlasting relief, someone must have heard her. It shouldn't have worked but by some miracle, it did. At the next rut, she pushed harder with her shoulder, pounding with every ounce of strength, and to her amazement, this time the bolt gave way and the doors flapped open.

Already in motion, Jane was unable to check her momentum. Newton's first law—an object in motion remains in motion—and all that. Even Harry Withington's daughter couldn't fight the laws of physics. Her arms flailing for balance, she tumbled out the open doors of the lorry at an awkward sideways angle.

Nor could she catch herself in time to avoid the rugby-ball-size rock wedged into the dirt road.

Her head connected with a hollow thud and the terrifying Utah mountains faded to black.

For a man who had spent most of his adult life staring into the gaping maw of danger, dealing with two little kids ought to be a piece of cake.

So why did he feel as if every step he took led him further and further into a hazardous minefield of emotion? Mason Keller wondered as he gazed at the girl and boy in the seat next to him in his pickup truck, one so grave and quiet, the other fidgeting like he'd just sat in a nest of fire ants.

"English, Charlie," he told the wiggler, trying his best to keep the weariness out of his tone at having to issue the too-frequent reminder to the boy again.

Charlie Betran sighed heavily, as if he carried the weight of the world on his narrow shoulders.

"Yes, sir. I forget," he said, each word precise and carefully enunciated.

"I know you do. You're doing great, though." Mason's smile encompassed both of them. Charlie smiled back but Miriam just gave him her usual solemn gaze.

Maybe he shouldn't push the two so hard to learn English. He could speak their native language, if not fluently, at least conversationally. But he knew Charlie and his older sister Miriam would be in for a mighty lonely existence if they couldn't communicate with their peers by the time school started in a few months.

"Why do we go on this road?" Charlie asked in English. "It is bumpy like a goat trail."

"I told you earlier. We need to check on my cattle grazing up here and then we're going fishing."

"Why?"

The kid's favorite question, in English or in Tagalog. He had become mighty damn tired of that question in the last three weeks since he'd managed to bring them out of the Philippines—and the two months before that, spent doing his best to get them all to this point.

Mason swallowed his sigh as his fingers tightened on the steering wheel. He could spot a hostile operative in a crowd of a thousand people, could sniff out a few ounces of plastic explosives like a bloodhound, but he felt like a complete idiot when it came to dealing with these children.

"It's fun, that's why. Trust me, you'll like it."

He hoped.

It was worth a try anyway. He had vivid memories of early-summer fishing trips with his own father up here amid the aspens and willows. Here in the Uinta Mountains was where he and his father connected best—one of the only places they managed that feat—and he supposed on some level he hoped he and Charlie and Miriam could forge the same bond.

He and the kids had to build a life together somehow. For the last ten weeks they had tiptoed around each other, afraid to breathe the wrong way, and it had to stop.

Mason was uncomfortable with children, especially *these* children. Whenever he looked into their dark eyes, he couldn't help thinking about Samuel and Lianne, their parents—two of the most courageous, most honorable people he had ever been privileged to know.

Assets, the intelligence community called them, but they were far more than that. They were friends, friends who risked their lives for years so they could feed him vitally important information about terrorism activity in their country.

He knew he shouldn't have come to care for them, just as they knew the dangers going into it. When the pair began to suspect their carefully woven cover had begun to fray, Samuel had begged Mason for help in sneaking his family out of the country. He had tried, but in the end his superiors had said they believed the Betrans' worries were unfounded and they were too valuable where they were.

After all their years of service, the people they had risked their life to help had turned on them and Mason counted himself among that number. He had done nothing to help them. Guilt and fury still overwhelmed him when he thought of their violent deaths in a car bombing two months earlier.

He hadn't been able to help the parents, but he'd be

damned if he was going to leave Samuel and Lianne's children in some crowded, dirty Philippine orphanage.

What else could he do but bring them home to the Utah ranch where he'd been raised?

He'd hoped that after a few months as the children's guardian he would be better at the job but he still felt as stiff and awkward with them as a squeaky new boot.

Miriam and Charlie would always grieve for their parents just as he would always be consumed with guilt over the deaths of his friends. But the three of them had to go on from here. They couldn't live in this tense détente forever.

The pickup hit a rut on the dirt road and jostled them all together. Miriam's eyes widened nervously but Charlie giggled.

"I like this bumping. It tickles here," the boy said, pointing to his stomach.

Mason summoned a smile. "You're a little daredevil, aren't you? You ever been on a roller coaster?"

He had to laugh at the boy's blank look. He was trying to think if he'd ever heard a Tagalog word for roller coaster when Miriam sat forward suddenly.

"Sir! Look out!"

He jerked his attention back to the road, barely in time to slam on the truck's brakes. The big three-quarter-ton pickup fishtailed to a stop just inches before he would have plowed over a woman lying in the middle of the dirt road, as if it was the ideal spot to take a little nap.

What in the hell?

He gazed through the windshield at the woman, but she didn't move even with the growling diesel engine practically crawling up her ear.

"She is dead, yes?" Miriam asked. There was resignation in her voice and Mason's jaw clenched. The girl had become obsessed with death since her parents had been killed. He supposed it a natural byproduct of what she'd been through but it still broke his heart.

"I don't know. I'll find out, though," he promised. "You two stay right here. Don't move."

He repeated the command in Tagalog to make sure they understood before he unlocked the jockey box for his Ruger and then stuffed in a couple of cartridges.

The woman didn't move even when he shut the door with a loud thud that seemed to echo in this quiet solitude. He approached warily, his weapon ready at his side. He might be overreacting, but a man with his life experience didn't take stupid chances.

One of the first rules of espionage. Anything out of the ordinary attracted attention, just as it should. And a woman lying in the middle of such an isolated mountain road was pretty damn extraordinary.

She definitely wasn't dead. Though she was laid out just like a corpse in a casket, her slight chest beneath her folded hands rose and fell with each breath.

She wasn't a hiker who had fallen, he saw as he approached. Not in those sandals and those dressy summer slacks. He scanned the mountains, looking for any sign of what might have brought her here. A car, a bicycle—a helicopter, for Pete's sake—but he saw nothing but trees.

Mason turned back to the woman, cataloguing her pretty features with dispassionate eyes. She looked to be mid- to late-twenties maybe, Caucasian. She had straight brown hair with streaky blond highlights, a small straight nose, a generous mouth, high cheekbones—one of which had traces of dried blood, he noted.

He did a quick visual scan for more injuries but couldn't see anything from here.

What was she doing here? He looked around again, his shoulder blades itchy. This would be a hell of a place for an ambush, isolated and remote enough to leave no witnesses.

Good thing there were no rebel fighters hanging out in Utah. Nothing stirred here but a few magpies chattering nearby and the wind moaning in the tops of the trees and fluttering the bright heads of the wildflowers that lined the road.

Still on alert, he engaged the safety on his weapon and shoved it into the waistband of his Levi's at the small of his back, then crouched near her and picked up one slim hand.

"Ma'am? Are you all right?" An inane question, he thought, even as he asked it. She obviously *wasn't* all right or she wouldn't be lying in the middle of an isolated mountain road.

She didn't respond so he gave her shoulder a little shake. That seemed to do the trick. The woman opened her eyes. They were blue, he noted. The same clear, vivid blue of the columbines growing wild all around them, and fringed with thick dark lashes.

She stared at him for just a moment and blinked a few times with a vague kind of look and then she smiled. Not a casual smile but a deep, heartfelt, where-have-you-been kind of smile and Mason wondered why he felt as though he'd just been punched in the stomach.

He had thought her pretty at first glance but with that smile, she was stunning.

"Hello," she said in a voice that sent chills rippling down his spine. If he were the kind of man who had ever had any inclination to try phone sex, he had a feeling her voice would have been just the thing to make him hotter than a two-dollar pistol—low, a little raspy, and sheathed in an oh-so-proper British accent.

His sudden, unexpected reaction to that smile and that sexy voice ticked him off. He rose to tower over her, angry at himself for his loss of self-control and at her for being the catalyst.

"You want to tell me what you're doing out here? I just about ran you over, lady. Don't you think you could have found a better place for a nap than the middle of the frigging road?"

She blinked at his harsh tone, then her eyes shifted to look around at the sage-covered mountains, the scattered stands of towering pine, the dusty road that stretched over the horizon, the complete absence of anything resembling civilization, except for one big rumbling pickup truck.

The woman's gaze shifted back at him and the blank, baffled expression in her eyes raised the hairs at the back of his neck.

"I don't know what I'm doing here," she whispered. "I don't even know where *here* is."

"You're in the middle of the Uinta Mountain Range."

"Wh-where is that?"

He frowned. What the hell was going on? "Utah. About an hour east of Salt Lake City."

Those blue eyes widened. "Why, that can't be possible. I've never been to Utah in my life. Have I?"

He raised an eyebrow. "Though I just set eyes on you five minutes ago and have no idea where you have and haven't been, ma'am, I'm going to take a wild guess here and say a big yes to the Utah question. See that license plate on my truck?"

Her gaze shifted from him to his pickup and he saw the

beginnings of unease stir on her expression. "What am I doing here? In *Utah?*"

With that upper-crust British accent, she made the word sound like a distant planet. A bizarre foreign planet in some galaxy far far away.

"I believe that was my question," Mason growled. "Why don't we start with your name."

The blank gaze shifted back to him. "My…name?"

Okay. He did *not* need this, one more complication in an already entangled life.

"Your name. First name. Last name. Anything."

"I…I don't know."

"Seems to me you don't know much," he snapped.

She scrambled to her feet, the beginnings of panic in her eyes. As she rose, he saw she was no taller than perhaps five foot four, slender and fragile-looking, especially with the dried blood on her cheek.

She was obviously injured somehow, he reminded himself. And he was interrogating her like she was some kind of enemy combatant. He moderated his tone. "Are you hurt anywhere besides your face there?"

She pressed a slim hand to her cheek and then to the back of her head as if she'd only just realized it ached. When she pulled her fingers away he saw more dried blood on her fingers.

"Let me see." He stepped closer for a better look and she instinctively retreated from him, but she had nowhere to go with a throbbing pickup behind her.

He cupped her cheek in one hand and turned her head with the other. He was no medic but every intelligence agent had at least the bare bones of triage experience.

She had a nasty cut and what felt like a hell of a goose

egg at the back of her head, just above where neck met skull. A head injury could explain the apparent memory loss, if that's really what was going on here. If this wasn't some elaborate ploy.

Why would anybody go to all this trouble to stage an accident? he wondered. He'd been in the game so long he suspected everybody of deception and subterfuge.

He was going to have to take her to help. Even if he didn't completely trust her, he couldn't leave a woman out here alone. It might be hours—or even days—before another vehicle traveled through this remote area.

Before he could explain that to her, he heard a truck door shut and he had time only for one bitter curse as Miriam and Charlie peeked around the pickup, anxiety in their dark eyes.

"Didn't I tell you two to wait in the truck?" Mason asked. Was there not one part of his life under his control?

"Charlie was scared," Miriam said in her native language. By the shadows in her eyes, he could see her little brother wasn't the only nervous one. "We wanted to make sure the lady was all right."

"I'm just fine," his mystery Brit answered in perfectly accented Tagalog, smiling at the children. "And how are you?"

He stared at her. "You speak Tagalog?" he asked incredulously. What were the odds of finding a woman in the middle of a deserted Utah road who spoke the children's language? This whole thing was beginning to seem more and more bizarre.

"Do I?"

He growled low in his throat in frustration. "You just did! How is it you know how to conjugate verbs in a foreign language but you apparently don't know your own damn name or why you're lying in the road in the middle of nowhere?"

She gazed at him, her blue eyes wide, distressed for several moments, with only the sound of his rumbling truck to break the vast silence, then he saw those eyes cloud with dismay and fear as the full reality of her situation soaked in.

"I don't know. I can't remember!"

Chapter 2

Panic was a wild creature inside her, clawing and fighting to break free. She stared at the stranger watching her through dark, suspicious eyes. He was so big, at least six foot two. The cowboy hat and the hulking, rumbling truck behind him somehow made him seem bigger, huge and dangerously male.

She had a funny feeling she didn't particularly care for large men. Or men who frowned at her with such ill-concealed vexation bordering on outright hostility.

She climbed to her feet as pain sliced through, making her head throb and spin like a whirligig. Despite the change in altitude, the man still towered over her.

"Are you telling me you don't remember your own name?" he asked, his voice as hard as the mountains around them. Her splitting headache kicked up a notch and she was afraid wild hysteria loomed on the not-so-distant horizon.

She screwed her eyes shut as if she might find the answer emblazoned on her eyelids and searched her mind for any snippet of information, no matter how tiny. All she found there was a blank, vast field of nothing.

No name, no age, no nothing.

"What's wrong with me?" she wailed. "Why can't I *remember?*"

The two children exchanged a nervous look at her outburst. Though she regretted scaring them, she couldn't seem to focus on anything but the pain in her head and her own burgeoning panic.

"Don't cry." The little boy spoke in Tagalog as he patted her hand. "It will be okay. You'll see. Mr. Mason will make it all better."

How perfectly ridiculous that she could find such comfort from this funny little creature with dark eyes and a winsome smile, but she couldn't seem to help it.

"Miriam," the American said in English, his voice deep and somehow calming, despite the suspicion in his eyes, "take Charlie to the truck and wait there. We'll be along in a minute."

The girl nodded and grabbed the boy's hand, tugging him toward the pickup. She watched them climb inside the big cab, already missing the buffer they provided between her and this angry-looking stranger.

"What's happened to me?" she asked when she was once more alone with the man. "Why can't I remember anything?"

His silver-gray eyes narrowed with mistrust. "If this is some kind of game, lady, you won't get away with it. I find you're trying to play me, and you can bet I'll be on you like a magpie on a June bug."

She wasn't sure what a magpie or a June bug might be but she sensed the metaphor wasn't intended to be pleasant. "It's not a game, I swear to you. I can't remember anything."

"You don't have the first clue what you're doing out here miles from anywhere? Come on. Think."

She would like to, but her brain seemed to have gone on holiday. Maybe she could hold a coherent thought if it weren't for the excruciating pain squeezing her skull.

She wanted nothing so much as to curl up again in the dirt until everything disappeared—the noisy truck growling behind her, this terrifying, suspicious American, and especially the hot stab of pain searing her skull.

"I don't know," she whispered. "I told you that. Why won't you believe me?"

He appeared to consider her question. "I'm not sure about the U.K.," he finally said, his voice dry, "but here in America women don't just drop out of the sky. How did you get here?"

All she wanted was a lie-down. Her head seemed to be inhabiting another postal code entirely from the rest of her body and she absolutely did *not* want to be standing here in the middle of the wilderness exchanging words with an arrogant cowboy who seemed determined to think the worst of her.

"I don't know," she repeated, pain and frustration and that skulking panic making her testy. "Perhaps I was abducted by little green spacemen who sucked out my memory before conking me on the head and tossing me out of their flying saucer."

He gazed at her out of those suspicious gray eyes for another moment and then she could almost swear she saw fleeting amusement flicker in his expression. At this point, she wasn't sure she really cared. Her small moment of defiant sarcasm seemed to have sapped her last bit of energy. She could feel herself sway and took a deep breath, forcing her knees, spine and shoulders to stiffen on the exhale.

"I'm sorry to have troubled you." She tried for as much dignity as she could muster. "If you could be so kind as to point me in the direction of the nearest town, I'll just be on my way."

He stared at her in disbelief for about half a minute then shook his head. "The nearest town is about seven miles that way on a dirt logging road. You really think you're up for that kind of hike in your condition?"

Daunted but determined, she nodded. "Certainly."

She could only wish her knees weren't so damned wobbly and her head wasn't throbbing like a finger slammed into an automobile door. She managed to take about five shaky steps before the American gave a put-upon sounding sigh and scooped her into his arms.

Her head whirled as the rapid shift in position exhausted all remaining equilibrium.

"Excuse me!" she still managed to exclaim hotly.

"You really think I'm going to let an injured, delusional Brit loose in these mountains? You need a doctor."

She opened her mouth to argue, but she couldn't seem to form any coherent thought, not when the cowboy held her so close. Heat radiated from him and he smelled earthy and masculine, of leather and sandalwood and something else ineffable.

Anyway, it was ridiculous to squabble with the man, especially when he was perfectly right. She wasn't sure she could have made it another step, much less trudged seven miles to the nearest town.

Her eyes drifted closed as he carried her to the large vehicle. Though she told herself it was to hold the vertigo at bay, in truth she was aware of a wonderful—but supremely foolish—sense of safety in his arms.

The cowboy opened the passenger door to the lorry and ordered the children to slide over, then set her inside with a careful gentleness that for some ridiculous reason brought tears to her eyes.

"Thank you," she whispered.

He paused, studying her with an inscrutable look, then with an odd sigh he closed the door, walked around the vehicle and climbed inside. He worked the gears and the lorry surged forward. A moment later he had turned the huge beast around and they were headed in the opposite direction.

They rode in silence for several long moments. Through the ache in her head, she was aware of furtive looks sliding in her direction with some frequency from the two younger occupants of the vehicle.

They were darling children, small and slender with huge dark eyes. Given their use of Tagalog, she had to assume they were Filipino and she wondered what they were doing with this large, formidable man.

"I am Miriam Betran," the girl said after a few more moments. She spoke in solemn, careful English, as polite as if she were performing introductions at a garden party. "This is my brother, Charlie. I am nine, he is only five."

"Almost six," the little boy piped up.

"Hello," she replied, wishing she had some kind of name to offer in return.

"Our mama and papa are dead. Mr. Mason says he is our papa now. That is why we come to United States."

She shifted her gaze to Mr. Mason and saw a muscle twitch in that masculine jaw. He offered no explanation and she couldn't summon the energy to request one, even if any of this had been her business.

"Thank you for helping me, Mr. Mason," she said instead.

"Just Mason. Mason Keller."

"Are you a cowboy, Mr. Keller?"

His mouth curved slightly. "Something like that. My family ranch is on the other side of these mountains."

"I'm sure it's lovely," she murmured.

"I don't know about that. Mostly sagebrush and dust. But I like it."

She wanted to answer but couldn't seem to make her brain communicate with her mouth to squeeze the words out. She also couldn't for the life of her figure out why she was so drowsy suddenly but her eyelids seemed to weigh five stone each.

The urge to close them was overwhelming. Perhaps only for a moment, just long enough to ease the strain a bit....

She must have drifted to sleep. Her dreams were full of fear that tasted like bile in her mouth and the rapid pulse of blood through her veins. She needed to run, to get away. From what?

A sudden cessation of sound and movement finally awakened her, to her vast relief. She opened her eyes and found her escort had parked before a small single-story building of pale-red brick. A carved wooden sign out front proclaimed the structure to contain the Moose Springs Medical Clinic. Below it was the name Dr. Lauren Maxwell.

"She is awake, I think," the boy pointed out, peering around his sister to be sure.

"Yes. I'm awake. I'm sorry I fell asleep."

"It would really make my day if you could tell me you woke with crystal-clear memory of who you are and what you were doing in the Uintas," Mason Keller said.

She poked around in her mind again but found it empty beyond that moment earlier when she had opened her eyes and found him staring down at her. That beastly panic returned to gnaw at her control. "No," she whispered, her head still pounding.

He blew out a resigned breath. "Yeah, I figured that's what you'd say. Let's go see if Lauren can fix you up."

"The doctor is nice," Charlie confided in Tagalog. "She gives candy if you do not cry."

She had to smile at the little boy, despite the nerves fluttering in her stomach. "I'll try not to cry, then," she responded.

The something-like-that cowboy climbed out of the truck then moved around to her side to open the door. He reached a hand inside to help her out and she had to admit she was grateful. Without his assistance she would have stumbled on knees that seemed as wobbly as a bowl of pudding.

The medical clinic was airy and bright, painted a cheerful yellow. The reception area seemed empty of patients but two women stood talking behind a desk, a matronly brunette who looked to be in her fifties and one at least a couple of decades younger, wearing jeans and a casual T-shirt.

She would have guessed the older woman to be the doctor but soon learned her error. The young woman's features lit up when she saw Mason and the children, and she came out into the reception area through a door to the left of the desk.

She smiled at the children, touching Miriam gently on the shoulder. "Hey, kids. Great to see you again!"

The girl gave her a tiny smile in return, but Charlie turned suddenly shy, hiding behind the tall cowboy.

"Who's your friend, Mase?" the woman asked.

"Hey, Lauren." He stepped forward and kissed the lovely young woman on the cheek. "I brought you a little business. Jane Doe. The kids and I found her up in the Uintas. Damnedest thing. She was just lying in the middle of the logging road up near Whitney Reservoir. Claims she doesn't remember who she is or how she got there."

Beside him, her spine stiffened at his choice of words and the inherent suspicion in them. "I *don't* remember! Why on earth would I lie?"

He ignored her heated defense of herself as if she were an annoying little bug. "I did a little triage on the scene. Looks like she cut herself somehow on her face—a while ago, I'd guess, judging by the dried blood—and she's got a heck of a goose egg on the back of her head."

"But no ID?"

"Nothing. No car, no purse, no nothing, at least not that I could see. I didn't reconnoiter the whole area, though. I'm wondering if she might have taken a wrong turn up there somewhere, then had an accident and wandered away from the scene."

"What a mystery." The doctor gave her a curious look that made her feel a bit like a primate in a zoo exhibit.

"She seems to think little green men in a spaceship dropped her off," Mason said.

"I do not!" she exclaimed. "I was merely responding to your suspicions with sarcasm."

For some reason, that seemed to amuse him. A corner of his mouth lifted then he turned back to Dr. Lauren Maxwell. "On the way out of the mountains I put in a call to

Daniel, since mysterious Brits with head injuries are his territory. He should be here any minute. I figured maybe you could check her out in the meantime, see if anything's permanently busted."

"Of course." The physician gave her a friendly smile that was undoubtedly meant to be reassuring. "I'm sure everything will be just fine. Let's get you cleaned up, shall we?"

She studied the other woman, but she couldn't seem to make herself move, reluctant suddenly to leave Mason Keller's side.

How perfectly ridiculous. She didn't even know the man and what she *did* know, she didn't particularly care for. He was dictatorial to the children and had treated her with nothing but harsh suspicion since stumbling upon her.

She knew she was being silly to cling to him but he and his Tagalog-speaking children were the only relatively known commodity in her world right now and she couldn't bear the thought of leaving his side. What if he left her here?

When she couldn't seem to make her legs cooperate to follow the young physician, Mason turned to her. For the first time since he'd found her, his gray eyes softened and his expression seemed to relax slightly. She blinked at him, disoriented. Why did he suddenly look so familiar?

"Go on," he urged quietly. "We'll wait out here until you're done."

"Promise?" She despised the slight quaver in her voice but couldn't seem to help it.

"Stick a needle in my eye."

Slightly reassured, she followed the young doctor down a hallway to a small examination room painted in a soothing blue and decorated with dried flowers and a pile of magazines stored in what looked to be a large antique washbasin. There was a mirror in the room above the sink and she had the disconcerting realization that she had no idea what kind of reflection she would encounter there.

The doctor gave her a friendly smile and pulled a hospital gown from a drawer built into the examination table. "So you have no memory of your name or anything?"

She shook her head, embarrassed and afraid all over again.

"Mason called you Jane Doe. Do you mind if I call you Jane until we find out your real name? It's better than 'hey, you' and that way I'll have something to put on your chart."

The name didn't seem *wrong*, exactly, so she nodded. In an odd way, it actually felt good to have a name to hang on to, even if it wasn't the correct one. "Jane is fine," she murmured.

"Good. And you can call me Lauren, all right?"

She nodded.

"Okay, Jane," the doctor said. "Let me wash my hands then we'll get started. Have a seat."

She climbed onto the examination table and had time to wonder how she could possibly know that contraption hanging on the wall was called a blood pressure cuff but she couldn't remember her own bloody name.

"All right, then, let's take a look."

Jane sat quietly while the doctor looked her over. "This cut on your face looks superficial," she said. "I imagine it stung quite a bit but I don't believe you'll have a scar. I think I'll order a tetanus shot under the circumstances, just to be safe."

The doctor shifted attention to the bump on her head and Jane couldn't contain a gasp at the pain at her gentle probing.

"I'm sorry. I'll leave it alone now." She stepped away.

"You said you don't remember anything at all before Mason found you?"

Terror.

The bitter, metallic taste of fear in her mouth.

I have to get out of here. Help me. Oh, help me.

The impression slammed into her out of nowhere. She caught her breath, grateful she was sitting down.

"No," she finally managed, frightened by the strength of the memory but somehow loathe to share it with the other woman.

The doctor studied her. "You're obviously British, though you might be an expatriate, I suppose. Do you have any idea at all what you might be doing in our little neck of the woods?"

"No. It's as if there's a huge closet in my mind with all those memories jumbled away. I know it's there. It has to be. But I can't manage to fit the right key."

She paused, then finally voiced the question that had haunted her since she'd opened her eyes on the road and found Mason Keller standing over her. "Doctor, will I ever remember?"

"I'm afraid I can't give you a straight answer to that. All I can tell you is that you appear to have suffered a nasty head injury. It wouldn't be unusual for such an injury to result in some degree of memory loss, but whether that's permanent or not, I can't say. I'm sorry."

Jane hugged her arms around herself, cold suddenly even though the room's temperature was comfortable.

"Let's not get ahead of ourselves, though. I'd like to take an X-ray and possible CT scan, just so we know for sure what we're dealing with, all right?"

Jane nodded, though she doubted any medical test could explain away the fear that seemed to simmer just below the surface.

"It sure is good to have you back in town, Mase." Lauren's receptionist Coralee Jenkins beamed at him, her wide features friendly and open. "I know you were doing important work in the military—your dad was mighty proud of you for it—but we missed you while you were gone."

Mason had to force himself to smile politely. The last topic of conversation he wanted to dig into was what he'd been doing with himself while he was away from Moose Springs.

He had always liked Coralee. He'd even dated her daughter for a few months back in high school, and Coralee and her husband Bruce had always gone out of their way to treat him better than an obnoxious punk like him had deserved.

Still, he had to wonder what Lauren's receptionist would have to say if he filled her naive little ears full of his real activities during the last dozen years instead of the politely vague cover he provided to family and friends.

In her quiet, safe world, she would probably never believe the kid who had stoically endured a thirty-minute lecture from Bruce after he'd returned Sherry home fifteen minutes past curfew could spend more than a decade submerged deep in a shifting world of lies and deceptions.

Coralee would understand little of that world—and he had to admit, that's just the way he liked it.

"How's Sherry these days?" he asked, keeping one eye on Charlie and Miriam watching a television set in the corner of the waiting room where SpongeBob SquarePants was frying up Krabby Patties.

The question diverted Coralee, as he'd hoped. Her eyes lit up and she reached for a framed photograph on her desk. She handed it over the counter to him and he studied the picture for any trace of the perky, flirtatious cheerleader he'd dated in the suburbanite who beamed back at him, flanked by a handsome balding man and a trio of red-haired kids. He couldn't see much resemblance to that girl he'd known, except maybe for a little devilish light in her eyes.

"Great," Coralee said with a proud smile. "Just great. Married to an Ob/Gyn in Utah County and she keeps plenty busy raising my three grandkids. Aren't they something? The baby just turned two. He's a handful, I'll tell you. Keeps her running all day."

She went on to detail Sherry's soccer-mom lifestyle that seemed completely foreign to him, but he surprised himself by managing to carry on a halfway coherent conversation anyway.

Adaptation.

That was the key to being a good counterintelligence agent. His first lessons after being recruited from the Army Rangers had focused on learning how to conform to his surroundings, to blend in and appear part of the landscape, whether that was a crowded Manila bar or a tiny fishing village in Mindanao.

He had been good at that part of the job. Whoever would have thought that subterfuge and deceit would come so naturally to a hick cowboy from Utah?

He had spent so long trying to be someone else, it was sometimes hard to remember who he was.

"Speaking of kids," Coralee said suddenly, "those sure are a couple of cute ones you brought back with you."

He ignored the blatant opening she gave him to spill the details he was sure she hankered after about Charlie and Miriam.

The Moose Springs gossip line was no doubt buzzing like crazy when he'd showed up after all these years with a couple of Filipino kids. A few trusted friends knew as much of the story as he could freely tell, but the rest of the town probably had all kinds of ideas about where Charlie and Miriam came from.

He had to wonder what the gossips would say when word got out that he'd found a mystery woman up in the mountains.

Somehow his plans to come back to a quiet, uneventful life on the ranch weren't exactly coming to fruition.

He was spared from having to come up with a polite answer to Coralee's conversational probe by the door opening. A moment later the Moose Springs sheriff sauntered inside, looking big, bad and hard as a whetstone.

The other man took one look at Mason and narrowed his gaze. "I should have known trouble would follow your sorry ass back to town."

Mason slowly straightened. "You got a problem with my sorry ass coming back to your town?"

His cool tone had the children looking up warily. Before he could reassure them, the sheriff's stern expression melted into a grin and he slapped Mason on the back, the male equivalent of a hug.

"Damn, it's good to see you, man!" Daniel Galvez exclaimed. "How long has it been? Three years? Four?"

"Something like that."

Mason hated that he had come to avoid his good friends over the years. Friends tended to ask the kinds of questions he couldn't answer honestly, like what he was doing with his life. Since he hated lying to his friends the way he did to everyone else, it had become easier just to stay away.

"How've you been?" he asked Daniel.

"Good." His grin slipped a little but Mason pretended not to notice. "Dispatcher tells me you've got a mystery on your hands."

"Not *my* hands. You're the law around here, hard as that still is for me to believe."

"That's what they tell me, anyway."

Mason quickly explained the events of the last three hours.

"Whereabouts did you say you found her?"

"I've got the GPS coordinates out in the truck. But you'll know where it is without them. Do you remember that time in high school we camped up near Sulpher Springs with Truman and Fricke? This was about a mile down from where we camped."

"Yeah, I know the area. Give me the coordinates and I'll send a deputy up there to see if he can find any kind of vehicle pulled into the brush or down a ravine or something. I can also check missing persons reports in the region, although it may be a day or two before anything turns up. What do you plan to do with her in the meantime?" Daniel asked.

Mason frowned at the odd question. "Do with her? Not a blasted thing. I drove her down the mountain for medical attention and brought in the authorities. As far as I'm concerned, my work here is done. I've got enough on my plate without adding this, too. I'm done with it. The woman is your problem now."

He heard a small noise in the doorway, just a strangled

gasp. He waited about five seconds, then shifted his gaze to the doorway where she stood, his Jane Doe, looking pale and fragile.

He had no doubt that she'd overheard his callousness, heard him referring to her like a piece of garbage nobody wanted.

Damn.

Chapter 3

"**I**'m sorry I've been such a bother to everyone."

That low, proper voice sent an oddly tangled shaft of guilt and heat through him. He didn't care for either emotion. He had no business being attracted to this woman, not when the only thing he knew about her was that he couldn't afford to trust her. And he certainly had nothing to feel guilty about, not when he had two children to protect.

"We all just want to help you, Jane."

While Lauren spoke to the mystery woman, the reproach in her eyes was for Mason alone.

"Jane?" Mason seized on the last part of Lauren's comment. "That's her name? Is she starting to remember?"

Lauren shook her head. "Not yet but we have to call her something. Jane fits as well as anything else."

He swallowed his oath as the physician greeted Daniel

with a cool wariness at odds with her usual cheerful demeanor. Where did that come from? Mason wondered.

He didn't have time to puzzle that out before the sheriff stepped forward, studying the mystery woman with interest.

"Hello." His pleasant smile seemed to put the mystery woman at ease. "I'm Daniel Galvez, the Moose Springs sheriff."

Mason watched closely for any sign of nervousness in her expression, the usual telltale signs of a person who might have something to hide from law enforcement. She was good, he'd give her that much. If she was hiding something, she didn't betray it by so much as a blink.

"What did the examination show?" Daniel asked.

Lauren's mouth tightened and Mason thought for a moment she wouldn't answer him, then she shrugged. "The CT scan showed a definite head injury, relatively mild but still serious enough to warrant close observation. I don't believe she needs to be hospitalized at this point, however."

"What about the amnesia?" Mason asked. Is it real or some kind of scam? he thought but didn't add.

"Memory loss is certainly a possible side effect of her kind of head injury."

"Temporary or permanent?"

Lauren gave her patient a quick sidelong look, then shifted her gaze to his and he couldn't miss the warning signals there for him to have a little more tact.

"At this point it's too early to answer that with any degree of certainty. I have every reason to believe it's a temporary condition but I can't say how long that particular side effect may linger."

"Can you give a ballpark figure?"

"No," Lauren said firmly.

"Did you find any identifying features?" Daniel broke in. "A tattoo or a scar or anything?"

The doctor shook her head. "She seems in good condition. Other than the cut on her cheek and a little bruising on her arms, she doesn't have any other injuries. I did find evidence of a broken arm that was poorly set and a couple of fingers that have been broken in the past but that's all."

Daniel wrote that down. "What about age, height, weight? Any idea?"

"I would guess her age somewhere between twenty-five and thirty." She glanced down at the clipboard in her hand. "Five feet three inches tall and a hundred ten pounds."

"You all do know I'm standing here, don't you?" Jane asked suddenly, her voice tart and her cheeks slightly pink.

Lauren winced. "I'm sorry. We *were* talking about you a bit as though you weren't here, weren't we? Do you have any other questions?"

"No. I just want this to be over."

Daniel gave her a reassuring smile. "I'll put out some feelers, see if we can find out who you might be. Somebody's probably looking for you, and I doubt it will take long to solve this mystery. But in the meantime, we need to find somewhere for you to stay."

Daniel and Lauren turned toward Mason in unison, as if they were bobblehead dolls on the dashboard of a jacked-up GTO doing a fast turn around a corner.

He looked from first one to the other. "What? Why are you looking at me?"

"Finders keepers."

Despite the fact that Daniel was one of his oldest friends, Mason wondered if punching him would wipe that grin off his face.

"That's fine for pennies you pick up outside the hardware store," he muttered, "but not so appropriate when it's a strange woman you're talking about."

"She has to stay somewhere. I can't put her in jail since she hasn't done anything wrong."

"Perhaps there's a hotel I could check into somewhere close by." Jane's features suddenly clouded over. "Though I suppose without a purse, I have nothing to pay them with, do I?"

Lauren shook her head. "Even if we had a hotel in town, I wouldn't be able to recommend that. You've had a head injury and while you don't need hospitalization at this point, you do need someone close by the next few days to keep an eye on you. I would take you to my house but I'm heading to a conference in Ogden for the weekend."

"And I'm working double shifts all week," Daniel added.

In desperation, Mason turned to Coralee, who had been eavesdropping shamelessly on the whole conversation. The receptionist shook her head firmly. "Sorry. No can do. Bruce and I are spending the weekend in Vegas for our thirty-fifth anniversary."

Damn. He was stuck with the woman. As if he needed a headache like this in his life right now.

"I'm sorry to be such a bother," she whispered again. To his dismay, her chin started to wobble a little and tears welled up in the depths of those blue eyes.

Mason frowned, horrified that all he seemed to want to do was wrap his arms around this small, fragile creature and pull her against him. Anything to keep those tears away.

He wasn't sure where all these protective impulses were coming from but he'd better do his best to get rid of them.

"I guess she can stay at the ranch for a few days." His

voice came out gruff but he was still rewarded with a pleased nod from Lauren, a measuring look from Daniel and a watery smile from Jane Doe herself.

At least at the ranch, he could keep an eye on the woman, he thought. He was a highly trained intelligence operative for the United States government. If she was up to something, he would do everything in his power to find out what.

The children were thrilled to have the woman they considered their own personal discovery riding home with them.

Charlie bounced in his seat and chattered a mile a minute to her in his native language and even Miriam consented to give a few hesitant smiles to their guest.

Those smiles made his gray mood even darker. It was all he could do to get the little girl to look at him, forget about smiling. This strange woman waltzes in and suddenly she becomes the children's best friend without even lifting a finger.

"We were going to catch a fish today but we found you instead," Charlie said in Tagalog.

"English," Mason said, a little more curtly than he intended. His reminder earned him long-suffering looks from Charlie and Miriam and a decidedly annoyed look from his mystery guest.

"What harm can it do for them to speak their native language?" she asked him quietly.

Mind your own damn business, he wanted to say. He wasn't about to get into this with her in front of the children—especially since Miriam, at least, understood a great deal more English than she let on.

He could smile, too, when the occasion called for it so he pasted a polite one on his face.

"Despite the fact that Tagalog speakers suddenly seem to be dropping out of the sky today," he said dryly, "for the most part no one around here will understand them if they don't learn English. They won't have friends and they won't be able to keep up in school. I've told them they can speak Tagalog to each other all they want but I want them practicing English with me and with others as much as possible before school starts."

She opened her mouth and he saw arguments brewing in her eyes. Don't do it, he thought.

He was in no kind of mood for a lecture and the last thing he needed was parenting advice from a stranger who claimed she didn't even know her own name. He felt inadequate enough about this whole fatherhood gig. He didn't need her making it worse.

Instead, she surprised him. "Yes, I can see the wisdom in your approach," she murmured, her expression thoughtful. "I'm sure they will learn English more quickly and efficiently if it's spoken to them often. Being a child in a new country where one doesn't know the language can be quite lonely."

"How would you know that? The voice of experience?" Maybe this was a clue to her past, one he should mention to Daniel.

Her brow furrowed and he could almost see her trying to concentrate. "I don't know, precisely. Just an impression."

Mason seemed content to let the matter drop, to her vast relief. Trying to probe around in her mind only made her head throb with tension. Still, she couldn't seem to keep from it. Without a past, she had nothing. She *was* nothing.

She forced her mind away from those kinds of grim thoughts and turned her gaze out the window, letting Charlie's aimless, cheerful chatter soothe her spirit.

They drove through a raw-looking landscape of foothills covered in little more than a silvery-green brush—sage? she wondered—and dust. The landscape seemed huge here, wild and almost savage. If not for the occasional vehicle passing in the other direction, she would have thought they were alone out here save for the cattle; huge dark beasts contained by rusty barbed-wire fences.

This all seemed so alien to her, vaguely frightening in its vastness and isolation. She had to wonder if the strangeness of it was due to her memory loss or whether she would have found it disconcerting even if she remembered everything.

It was wild and harsh-looking, she thought after a few more moments of gazing out the window, but there was a raw and almost painful beauty to the landscape.

"Can you tell me where we are?" she asked after a moment. "I seem to remember something you said earlier about Utah, but would you mind perhaps being a little more specific?"

The look Mason sent her was full of suspicion. What made him so mistrustful? she wondered. Was it something about her or did he behave that way with everyone? It seemed a dreadful way to live, if the latter was the case.

"The town you just left is Moose Springs, population about three hundred, give or take a few," he said after a moment. "We're about an hour northeast of Salt Lake City."

Useful information, she thought. If only she knew anything about Salt Lake City.

"The ski resort community of Park City is just over those mountains as the crow flies but more like a half-hour if you're in a car," he went on. "The road we found you on was inside the Uinta Mountain Range, in the Wasatch-

Cache National Forest, a vast tract of land that includes a wilderness area of about half a million acres."

For some reason, her stomach clenched at that. She had a feeling she wasn't particularly enamored of anything with the word *wilderness* in its descriptor.

"And where are we going now?" she asked.

"My family's ranch, the Bittercreek. It's about three miles out of town. We should be there in a minute."

She had the sudden disquieting thought that she was traveling with a man she'd known less than a few hours to stay with him at his ranch, out in the middle of nowhere. She knew nothing at all about him. Perhaps she might have been better to throw herself on the mercy of the law officer back at the clinic.

"Mr. Mason, he has many of the horses and cows," Charlie Betran said in his careful English.

"They are very big," Miriam added.

"You'll get used to them," Mason said to the girl with a surprising gentleness. "Like I've told you, once you've been here awhile you won't be so nervous around them. I know you'll like the horses once you let me take you for a ride. Charlie likes them, don't you, bud?"

The boy nodded his head vigorously, beaming at Mason.

What was the story here, she wondered. Why did this strong, masculine cowboy have custody of these two children who seemed so far from home? They seemed such an odd mix for a family.

At least they had each other.

She had no one, she thought. At least no one she remembered. What a demoralizing thought. Could she have a child somewhere? A husband who might be looking for her?

Helpless frustration washed through her and she let out

a long breath. The lovely physician had said her memory
would likely come back in a few days. She had to hang on
to that hope. Worrying about something she couldn't control would accomplish nothing and would only make her
ill from the effort.

Dr. Maxwell said she needed to give herself time to
heal and she resolved to do just that.

A few moments later, Mason turned the vehicle under
an archway constructed of two massive upright logs topped
by a horizontal one just as big with the word *Bittercreek*
carved into it in letters that had to be at least two feet high.

The rather grand sign out front turned out to be fancy
wrappings for old rubbish, she discovered as he drove up
a long winding driveway. She was surprised to find Mason
Keller's ranch had a tired, worn-out feel to it—weathered
outbuildings in want of paint, sagging fencelines, old
rusted farm machinery hulking in fields.

Odd, that, when the vehicle they were riding in smelled
new and had to have cost him a pretty penny.

Perhaps he spent all his money on vehicles—and on
adopting two Filipino children.

The ranch house squatted square and solid at the end of
the long gravel driveway. It looked to be two stories, with
a trio of gables and a porch that stretched across the entire
width of the house. The whole thing was painted a bright
white that gleamed in the hot afternoon sun, even though
she could see it needed a fresh coat.

Someone was making an effort to spruce up the place,
she thought, if the raw plywood and cans of paint on the
porch were any indication.

The children climbed out on the driver's side after
Mason but Jane remained seated.

She couldn't seem to make her muscles cooperate. Her head still pounded and she was suddenly exhausted by all that had happened to her since she'd opened her eyes and found Mason looming over her.

After a pause while they waited for her, Mason finally walked around the truck and opened the passenger door. "Are you coming?" he asked.

Heat scorched her cheeks. He must think her a total idiot, which she was. "Ah, yes. Thank you," she murmured.

She straightened her shoulders and slid out of the truck, where she wobbled just a little before finding solid ground.

"Welcome to the Bittercreek," Mason said. His features were sardonic but she thought she detected something else. Not quite embarrassment, perhaps, but something close to it. "I'm afraid the red carpet is at the cleaners."

"It looks very comfortable and the view is lovely."

"I would apologize that it's probably not what you're used to. But since you claim not to be used to anything, I guess it doesn't much matter how humble the accommodations might be, does it?"

"Anything will be fine." She wasn't at all sure how to respond to the low antagonism in his voice so she decided to simply ignore it. "You're very kind to take me in," she went on politely. "Especially as I know how inconvenient it must be."

A muscle tightened along his jawline but he said nothing to either verify or deny her statement. "Sorry about the dust. We're in the middle of about a hundred renovations. The place has been empty for a couple years and it seems like everything needs to be done at once."

Why had the ranch been empty? she wondered. Where had Mason and the children lived before they came here to open up the Bittercreek again? She didn't have a chance to ask before the children grabbed her hands, one on either side.

"Come, Jane." Miriam gave one of those rare smiles. "You may sleep in my room."

"That's not necessary," Mason said. "We can air out one of the empty bedrooms for her. There's plenty of room."

He led the way up the rickety porch steps to the front door and then inside. Instantly, the delicious scent of roasting meat and vegetables wafted to them.

Antimacassars spread across the backs of armchairs.

Tea in a silver pot gracing a carved wooden tray.

A plump striped cat sprawled out on a rug before a merry little fire to take the chill out of a damp and dismal afternoon.

The memories were tiny and fleeting, but they still stopped her in her tracks as she tried to pin them down.

"Everything okay?" Mason asked.

"I…yes. That smell seems very familiar, that's all."

He gave her an odd look. "Smells to me like Pam's making a pot roast for dinner."

"Pam? Is that your wife?"

A shout of laughter greeted her question. She followed the sound to its source and found a woman standing across the room. She was short and slightly plump with a wild, curling mass of vivid red hair in a shade that couldn't possibly be natural. The woman laughed again, her expression friendly and open as she walked into the room.

"Better not let my Burnell hear talk like that. Though he's never been the jealous type, he just might start if he thought a troublemaker like Mason Keller had designs on me."

"Jane, this is Pam Lewis. She and her husband own the closest ranch down the road a way and they've been running things over here for me for the last few years. She's helping me out with the kids and the cooking temporarily, until we find our feet."

The woman stepped forward with a smile. "You must be our Jane Doe. You're even prettier than I heard."

Mason raised an eyebrow. "The Moose Springs grapevine has certainly been busy."

"Mase, you know your sudden return to town is the most exciting thing to happen around here since Doolley Shaw hit the cold medicine a little too hard and drove his truck clean into the side of Ben Palmer's barn."

Pam grinned at him. "Anything you do starts tongues flapping. What do you expect the gossips to do when you show up at Lauren Maxwell's clinic with a beautiful mystery woman on your arm? The phone lines are bound to start buzzing."

"I figured I'd at least have an hour or so lead time."

She laughed. "Coralee called to give me fair warning the minute you pulled out of the clinic's parking lot."

Mason's handsome features tightened into a grimace. "Surely there's something more exciting to gossip about."

She shook her head. "I, for one, don't know what that might be. I guess until Doolley gets the sniffles again, you're all we've got, boy. Better get used to it."

The woman shifted her attention to Jane and the amusement in her gaze gave way to compassion. "You poor little thing. You look dead on your feet. When was the last time you ate?"

Jane stared at her blankly and Pam slapped her forehead. "I'm such a dunce. You probably have no idea, do you? Well, are you hungry?"

She had to think about it. Though her stomach felt hollow, she wasn't sure she would be able to keep anything down with her head still throbbing. She had to try, though.

Common sense told her her body needed food to heal and she had a feeling her mind wouldn't heal until her body did.

"I am a little hungry," she admitted. "And I must say, your roast beef smells delicious."

"What you need is some food in your stomach and then a hot bath with a good book. I've got just the thing for you. Come on now, Auntie Pam will take care of you."

The woman looped her arm through Jane's and headed across the room. Left with little choice in the matter—and feeling rather as if she was caught in the whirl of a typhoon—Jane followed her with one last, bewildered look toward Mason.

Chapter 4

The Bittercreek ranch office was just down a short hallway from the kitchen. As Mason held the phone to his ear, waiting eternally on hold, he could hear through the open doorway the soft, musical voices of women and the occasional higher sounds of Miriam and Charlie chiming in.

He heard a small laugh, strangled before it really began, and realized it was Miriam's voice. How long had it been since she'd even attempted a laugh? he wondered. She had been a silent, watchful wraith since the day he'd showed up at her school in Butuan with the grim news about her parents.

He wanted fiercely to hear her give in to it. What would he give to hear her giggle and laugh like any other nine-year-old girl? Would that day ever come? She sure didn't laugh around him. She treated him with the same cool politeness he would employ with a slightly-less-than-adequate waiter.

The worst part was, he didn't have the first idea how to reach her.

He'd contacted a couple of grief counselors over the Internet and they'd both said it would take time for the children to adjust to their new life. In the blink of an eye, the spark of a fire to plastic explosives, their lives had changed completely.

They had lost everything they knew. First their parents had died and then he had dragged them away from all that was comfortable and secure, into a strange country with different customs and even a new language.

How could he blame Miriam for being slow to accept some of the changes in her life?

The music in his left ear continued to drone on. Over it, he heard Jane say something in that proper British accent, though he couldn't quite catch the words.

Low though it was, the sound of her voice seemed to slither through his skin and his insides clenched in response. This was getting ridiculous, he thought in disgust. It was only a voice. He had no business letting it slide across his nerve endings like a silk caress.

He couldn't trust her. This whole situation bugged the hell out of him. Yeah, she had a head injury. X-rays and CT scans didn't lie. But he still wasn't buying the whole amnesia story. It seemed entirely too unlikely.

What reason would she have for concocting the story, though? What could she be hiding? And how had she ended up on that mountain road in the first place?

His mind couldn't stop running through the possibilities, even as he waited on hold with the FBI. He couldn't help it. He'd been wading in counterintelligence waters too long to turn off the tap at will.

Scenario one, she'd had a car accident somewhere up in the mountains and wandered away from the scene, disoriented and injured. That could certainly be possible, but only if Daniel's deputies managed to stumble on to a damaged vehicle up there. Even if they did find a car, that still wouldn't explain why she might have been driving the dirt backroads of Utah in the first place.

Scenario two, this one a whole lot less palatable. Somebody who wanted to get rid of her whacked her over the head and left her for dead up in the mountains. She needed a convenient hiding place and found it here at the Bittercreek.

He didn't like considering that one. What could she have done to piss somebody off enough for that? If this theory were true, was anybody still looking for her? Was he placing the children in harm's way by allowing her to stay at the ranch?

He pushed that theory away as the telephone music changed to a murdered Elton John tune. He winced and went back to his speculations.

Scenario three was his least favorite. What if Jane was faking the whole thing—the head injury, the amnesia, everything—for nefarious reasons he couldn't quite work out yet?

He found it tough to reconcile the fragile, frightened-looking woman with someone who could carry out such a cold-blooded scheme, but those who could blend in and appear innocent on the outside always made the best operatives. Maybe she was just damn good at her job.

He had to admit, the whole thing smelled of a setup. But who could she be working for? Who would put so much time and energy into planting an operative on an isolated mountain road for the express purpose of having him find her?

He had more enemies than he liked thinking about—hostile operatives in organizations he'd worked to weaken like Abu Sayyaf and Jemaah Islamayah in the Philippines and similar groups in other countries, but also a few within the U.S. intelligence community.

His whereabouts were supposed to be a secret from all but the top echelons of the Agency but leaks were as common in the spy business as flies in a manure pit. A government can't expect to give its operatives the skills to infiltrate the organizations of enemy combatants without running the risk that they could turn those same skills inward and sneak through all the firewalls and safety nets.

He had angered a lot of people by dropping out of the Game. Mason couldn't deny that. He'd been a key operative in Mindanao and his cover had been solid. Though there were layers and contingency plans built into the system, his exit would certainly leave a void, one that hadn't gone over well with some.

As long as they kept their antagonism to themselves, Mason didn't care if the entire Agency had him on their shit list. He had given twelve years of his life to the cause—and most of his soul. Yes, he believed the work was important. Yes, he had played a valuable part in protecting the security of his country. But he had wondered for a long time—well before Samuel and Lianne were murdered—if the cost was worth it.

The music in his ear stopped abruptly and Mason sat up straighter.

"Hello?"

Finally, just when he'd been about ready to give up in disgust, he heard the slight West Texas twang of one of his FBI contacts in the Salt Lake City field office.

"Hey, Davis. Mason Keller."

Cale Davis had been sent to the Philippines as part of the FBI's Crimes Against Children unit. He was investigating a sex-slave ring where homeless Filipino kids were being sold to wealthy international businessmen. Though it wasn't typically his area of expertise, Mason, in his cover as an expatriate bar owner and sometimes arms trader, had found himself in a position to help the CAC investigation.

Their two worlds had collided and through it, he and Cale had somehow connected.

A long silence met his greeting and he could only guess what was running through the agent's mind.

"Keller," the other man finally said. "I've heard some interesting rumors about you."

"I can imagine."

"Did you really tell your division director to pull his thumb out of his ass before he dug around and found a terrorist cell up there?"

Mason grimaced. "Uh, something like that."

"Man, you always did have stones as big as watermelons. I heard you're gone from the Agency. Did they fire you?"

"I didn't give them the chance. I submitted my letter of resignation before that little altercation with my superiors."

"Why the grand exit?" Cale asked.

Mason thought of all the reasons he'd quit. The disillusionment. The grinding challenge of constantly playing a role, wallowing in filth and ugliness and unrelenting hatred every day of his life. The growing fear he was losing himself somewhere along the way.

Those were all secondary. He might have continued in counterintelligence forever, no matter the cost emotionally, if not for those two most important reasons now giggling in the kitchen with Pam and a strange Brit.

How to explain all this to Cale?

"Lianne and Samuel Betran are dead," he finally said. The other agent had met them during his time in the Philippines. Though he couldn't know the extent of their work for Mason, he would likely remember how instrumental they had been in his sex-ring investigation.

"I'm sorry," Cale said after a moment. "They were decent people. I know they were good friends of yours."

"They shouldn't have died." He pitched his voice low to ensure the children didn't inadvertently overhear. "Samuel came to me a week before they were killed. He wanted help smuggling Lianne and the kids out of the country. He was afraid their cover had been blown and his contact in the Jemaah Islamayah was beginning to suspect he was working with the Americans."

Acid washed into his stomach, as it did whenever he thought of the role he had played in their deaths with his helpless inaction.

"I tried to convince the brass but I couldn't get anybody to listen. The Betrans were too valuable where they were, they said. It was hellishly difficult to infiltrate the JI and any of their satellite organizations, and we would lose years of effort without Samuel in place. An extraction at that time wouldn't be in the best interest of our mission, they said."

"They were important assets in the region."

"They were people, damn it! A husband and wife who loved each other and their two kids, who thought they were doing something right and good. They believed in freedom and democracy and protecting the innocent and they spent ten years risking their lives for us! What did they get for it? When they needed help, we sacrificed them for the greater good."

He knew he sounded bitter but he didn't care. The fact that he couldn't really blame anyone but himself left more than acid in his gut. He should have tried harder, should have told his superiors to go screw themselves and helped the Betrans catch the next boat out of Butuan, no matter the cost to himself or the mission.

Every time he looked at those two orphaned children, his own failure to act haunted him.

"I'm sorry, man," Cale murmured.

"Yeah, me, too."

"I'm sure they weren't thrilled to lose you down there, too."

"Not my problem anymore." He couldn't let it be.

"I suppose that's true enough. So what are you doing with yourself?"

Besides failing completely as a father figure, trying to relearn ranching after years away from it and stumbling on to strange women up in the mountains?

"A little of this and that," he answered, loathe to explain to the agent about Miriam and Charlie. "You know I'm back in Utah, don't you?"

"I'd heard rumors. Something about a ranch in the family and you playing cowboy for a while. You're just over the mountains, right?"

Cale had been working out of the Salt Lake FBI field office for the last few years, precisely the reason Mason had tracked him down. "Yeah. Outside Moose Springs."

"Close enough to catch a beer sometime. Hope we won't run into any angry Filipino scooter gangs this time."

Mason laughed, to his great surprise. "Definitely. Next time I'm in the city, I'll call you." If he didn't have two little rugrats along, anyway.

"Listen," he went on, "I called because I need a favor."

"Anything. You know I'm in deep to you after you saved my ass in that bar in Tandag."

"I have no doubt you would have charmed your way out of it. It wasn't your fault you hit on the Vespa King's girlfriend."

He paused, trying to figure out the best way to explain about his Jane Doe. "Look, I know missing persons isn't your specialty—at least not missing adults—but I figured you could maybe keep your ear to the ground for me."

"About?"

He heard a small exclamation of laughter from the other room and somehow he knew it had to be Jane. The low, delighted sound seemed to slide down his spine, distracting him from his thoughts. He strained to catch more of it, or some clue into what might be so amusing, but couldn't hear anything future.

"About?" Davis prompted again after a moment.

"Sorry." He let out a breath and focused. "I need you to let me know if you hear any buzz about a missing persons case involving a woman—late twenties, maybe, with brown hair and blue eyes. British."

Cale said nothing for several seconds and Mason could almost hear his eyebrows rise. "Okay." The agent drew the word out. "You want to tell me what this is about?"

He sighed. "Long story, one I'm sure you'll never believe. I'll have to tell you over that beer."

"And in the meantime I'm supposed to keep my eye

open for a missing persons report. I don't suppose you might have a name to narrow things down. Quite a few missing persons reports pass through the field office."

"Negative on that. Only a description." Small, delicate. *Beautiful.*

"Of course not. A name would make things too easy, wouldn't it?"

The kitchen had fallen silent, he realized. A moment later he heard a flurry of footsteps going up the stairs. "I wouldn't need your help if I had a name."

"Right. Okay. I'll make a note of it. I can't make any promises. We're not always brought into missing persons cases and this one could slip through the cracks."

"That's all right. I appreciate your help."

They spoke a few moments longer about shared acquaintances. Cale told him he was off CAC for a while and working on other projects.

"You have to have a heart of iron to work Crimes Against Children all the time," he said.

"Yeah. I don't know how you've done it this long."

Even as he spoke, Mason found himself distracted, wondering what Jane and Pam and the kids were all doing up there. A moment later his question was answered when he heard the thump and moan of the pipes in the old ranch house and realized someone was running a bath upstairs in the clawfoot tub of the guest bathroom.

He had a quick mental image of that slender form slipping into warm, scented bubbles, all creamy skin and tantalizing curves. He lingered for only an instant on the image before he shoved it aside, disgusted with himself.

He was still castigating himself—and doing his best to

keep those images from reappearing—when he and the FBI agent ended their conversation a short time later.

"I'm sorry again about the Betrans, Keller," Cale said quietly. "I lost a partner a few years back. I was in a bad place for a long time, blaming myself, angry at the world. But I can tell you things do get better."

Did you have two constant reminders living with you? Mason wondered. Two children you didn't know what to do with, who cried in their sleep and looked at you out of dark, lost eyes?

"I'll keep that in mind," Mason murmured, then thanked the agent again for his help and hung up.

The water abruptly stopped and all was silent from up-stairs. It took every ounce of willpower not to dwell on those images of bubbles and curves again.

He was half-aroused, he realized with disgust. He had been without a woman far too long if he could get turned on trying *not* to imagine his mystery guest taking a bath.

He would have to do something about that, but he had no idea what. This was rural Utah. Unattached women willing to have a no-strings affair with a man who was lousy at relationships weren't exactly growing on trees in this region of the country.

In the meantime, he would have to just do his best to ignore his unwilling attraction to Jane Doe—and hope to hell he could figure out her game

After a delicious meal and a long, hot soak in water softly scented of lavender and chamomile, Jane felt almost human again.

Though her skin was wrinkled and pruney, the pervad-ing ache in her muscles eased and even the pounding in her head had dulled to a steady throb. Perhaps with a little sleep even that would fade.

She dried herself, dressed in the voluminous cotton nightgown loaned her by Pam Lewis, and found her way to the guest room Mason's housekeeper had pointed out.

The room was a little threadbare with only a bed, an old-fashioned carved chest of drawers and a small bedside table, but it was clean and comfortable enough and had a lovely view of the ranch and the surrounding mountains out the window.

All she really cared about was the bed, anyway. She wanted to sink into it and not climb back out for days.

She pulled back a pale-blue quilt of worn, soft cotton and slid between sheets that smelled of sunshine and fresh air. Ah, heaven.

Sleep didn't come immediately, despite her exhaustion. She couldn't have expected it to, not when her mind raced with a hundred questions. What was the story here with Mason and the children? How did a ruggedly handsome Utah rancher come to be the caretaker for two foreign-born children?

Why had his ranch been empty for the last few years? Where was he during that time and what had he been doing?

Why was he so suspicious of her, so unwilling to believe she was telling the truth about her amnesia? And why did he seem to be surrounded by a subtle air of danger, of keen alertness, as if he would be ready to take on any threat?

The more vital questions, of course, were the ones she almost couldn't bear entertaining.

Who was *she?*

What had she been doing on that mountain road?

What kind of life had she left behind?

Probing her mind for any clues only made her head begin to ache again. Perhaps it would be better to tuck those questions away for the morning and concentrate for now on sleeping, on giving her body a chance to heal.

Tomorrow could wait.

Simon Djami was not pleased.

He surveyed the four men in front of him, wondering why he had been cursed with such incompetence.

Fury whipped through him like the wind atop Mount Caragog, powerful and violent, but he allowed none of it to show through his supreme calm.

"I believe my instructions were quite simple," he murmured. "You were only to take the infidel woman into the mountains and kill her, leaving her in the most remote location you could find, a place where her carcass would not be discovered until long after our plans have come to fruition."

"Yes, sir. Those were your orders, sir." A tiny trickle of sweat dripped from the mustache of Ibram Ghalib and the man cast a nervous eye toward his three countrymen flanking him, as if he might deflect attention away from himself.

Foolish man. He was the leader. As such, he carried the responsibility for carrying out orders—and ultimately, the blame.

Simon would not let him take the coward's way out by turning that blame to others.

"Can you, great warrior, tell me why my orders were not obeyed?" Djami asked, his voice deceptively tranquil.

Ghalib seemed to relax, his coarse features losing some of their anxiousness.

"I cannot say, sir. We drove deep into the mountains but when we stopped, we discovered the woman was gone."

"Gone. Just like that? Is this woman an *aswani?*" He smiled as if the whole thing was a grand joke. "Do you think she performed some kind of evil magical spell and turned herself into a snake who could slither through her restraints and into the night?"

Ghalib, the stupid sod, laughed and the other idiots joined in. "As to that, I do not know, sir. We do know the doors to the truck were not latched properly. We believe she escaped that way. You can be assured, sir, that as soon as we discovered her missing, we tried to return the direction we had come to find her but these mountain roads have no signs. We drove all the night through but could not find her again."

Djami steepled his hands together. "This displeases me."

Ghalib bowed his head. "I am unworthy of your trust in me."

Yes. He had determined that already. Djami allowed a small portion of his terrible anger to show. "The woman is a threat to our entire plan. Only a handful of people in this cursed country speak Vandish and she is one. With all that she must have overheard, she knows everything. And now, because of your carelessness in letting her escape, one stupid female has the power to destroy many months of careful planning."

Ghalib swallowed hard, but he betrayed no other signs of nervousness.

"Have you forgotten our cause?" Djami went on. "The great splendor of Vandelusia? We must keep our beloved country pure and unsullied for our children and grandchildren. We cannot allow western infidels to bring their wicked dollars to corrupt our sons and defile our daughters, can we?"

"No, sir."

"We must stand together to defeat them." Djami allowed his voice to rise with passion. "If we allow the weak and manipulated leaders of our country to have their way, we will be forever allied with the evil infidels. We must fight for Vandelusia!"

Djami gauged his audience, saw the rising fervor on the features of all three men. "We have come too far to back down now. We cannot let one woman stand in the way of our plans. We must go forward to rid our country of this unholy influence forever!"

"Huzzah!" the men cried.

When their exultation had faded, he turned back to Ghalib. As leader of the VLF cell, he bore complete responsibility for failure.

"You do understand the importance of our mission, do you not, my friend?"

Ghalib nodded. "Yes, sir. Completely, sir."

"And yet you allowed the woman to escape, possibly to go to the inept and corrupt American police with lies."

"I am an unworthy servant. A thousand apologies."

Djami studied his henchman's bowed head with displeasure. This was not the first time he had encountered incompetence here. Ibram had passion in abundance but lacked vision and strength. The fool had been a stumbling block to his plans from the beginning.

"I'm afraid a thousand apologies are not enough, my friend." In one swift motion Djami pulled a small black Walther from the folds of his robe and squeezed the trigger.

Ghalib had time for only one tiny exclamation of surprise before he toppled back with a neat round hole in his forehead.

The other three men stared at Djami, their foolish eyes wide and terrified and their breathing harsh with fear.

He allowed himself a small smile. "Dispose of him and then find the woman, for the glory of Vandelusia. This time I would advise you not to fail."

Chapter 5

Fear had a bitter, metallic taste, almost like blood.

It welled up in her throat, thick and rancid, then spilled into her mouth until she couldn't breathe around it.

Something was out there. Waiting. Watching. Something dark and terrifying.

She wanted to run but she couldn't seem to make her arms and legs move. She was caught, she realized with horror—tangled in a silken web in a cage of metal that seemed to be in motion.

With every movement, each frantic effort to free herself, the strands binding her in place seemed to tighten until she was wrapped so tightly she could barely breathe.

Escape! She had to find a way to break free. She *had* to. Evil lurked just beyond her restraints. If she didn't escape and try to stop it, she and untold other innocents would be consumed in a thick cloud of choking smoke and poison.

But what could she possibly do? She was only one insignificant, cowardly female. Better to stay here. For now she was safe.

Not for long, she suddenly realized. Nowhere was free from its spreading, cancerous hatred.

The evil drew closer, until she could smell its fetid breath, feel the enmity blasting off it in hot waves. She cringed inside her silken trap, tried to draw herself into the tiniest ball as she waited for the final blow, yet still it moved closer and closer with a hideous, mocking laugh that seemed to go on forever.

"Please. Please, no," she whispered, then cried out just as the evil force reached out to pull her into the tight, suffocating embrace of death...

"Easy now. Everything's all right."

The voice was hard and masculine but seemed to wrap around her with the same warmth of the quilt covering her.

Jane blinked away the last dregs of the horrid nightmare and found Mason Keller standing next to the bed. She had left the bedside lamp on before she fell asleep, loathe to face the dark alone, and his features looked strong and commanding in the soft glow of its light.

"You were dreaming," he murmured. "A pretty nasty one, by the sound of it."

She shouldn't have found his voice so soothing, any more than she should have found such comfort in his presence. But seeing him standing beside the bed made the world suddenly seem not quite so dark and terrifying.

She closed her eyes. A nightmare. Those moments of terror were only her imagination. They couldn't possibly be real.

"Do you remember anything?"

She remembered cowering in fear as evil circled around her, ready to move in for the kill. Whether that memory was real or a figment of her imagination, she had no idea.

"I don't know," she murmured. "Only vague impressions."

"What kind of impressions?"

Her hands curled around the quilt as shame that seemed oddly familiar washed through her. "I was afraid," she admitted softly.

"I figured as much. You cried out."

She wanted to pull the quilt over her head and cringe with embarrassment. Having a nightmare in the first place was horrible enough but she felt invaded at the idea of someone else watching her and overhearing her private night terrors while she slept.

"Did I say anything?" She held her breath, horridly afraid of his answer.

For some reason she couldn't fathom, his gaze seemed to sharpen at her words and she felt rather like a bug under a magnifying lens.

"No words I could figure out, mostly gasps and cries," he said. "You did say 'please' and 'no' a few times but that was about it."

Well, that was a relief, she had to admit, though even now the dream seemed to be slipping away from her and she couldn't remember what could possibly have frightened her so much.

Perhaps that had to do with Mason's presence. Despite his continued mistrust of her, something about the man soothed her and comforted, inspired calm and peace.

She wondered if he realized he had an air of complete competence, that he could handle any challenges thrown his way. As long as he was near, she was safe. No one could possibly touch her while Mason Keller was around to protect her….

The thought made her frown. Protect her from what? Surely there was no threat to her safety. She'd had an accident in the mountains, that was all. Nothing to cause any alarm or this terrible nightmare.

"What else can you remember from the dream?" he pressed. "Any little detail might be enough to help us figure out who you are."

She didn't want to tell him anything. It all seemed so bizarre. Paranoid, even. Evil forces, choking clouds of poison. Surely it was only a nightmare. How could the bizarre workings of her subconscious mind possibly help him determine her identity?

She hesitated for just a moment longer, then slowly told him all she could remember. "I was somewhere dark and suffocating. Trapped. The air was stale and I couldn't breathe. I wanted to escape but I was afraid to leave. And then I woke. That's all I can remember."

"Nothing else?"

She decided not to tell him about the evil forces she felt gathering around her, the hatred and maliciousness. He would surely think her crazy if she spouted that kind of nonsense.

"That's all."

His eyes glinted silver in the low light as they narrowed at her. He studied her for a moment, long enough for her to begin to feel self-conscious of her borrowed nightgown, several sizes too large, hanging loosely.

Feeling foolish, she tugged up the neckline and searched for a distraction. "How did you know I was having a nightmare?" she asked.

He shrugged. "Lauren asked me to check on you. I've been coming in about every hour or so to make sure you're still breathing."

"Oh." The thought of him coming into her room while she slept and studying her with those silver-gray eyes was enough to leave her flustered, off-kilter.

She wasn't sure why she found the idea so disconcerting. Surely he wouldn't have tried anything untoward while she slept. But he was still virtually a stranger and she hated knowing she had been vulnerable, exposed to him without knowing it.

"Surely that wasn't necessary. I've been such a bother."

"No big deal. I was up, anyway."

She let out a breath, conscious of the debt she owed this stranger, despite her discomfort. "You've been more than kind, rescuing me today and then opening up your home for me to stay. I don't believe I ever said thank you. I'll say it now. Thank you, Mr. Keller."

He shrugged, though he looked uncomfortable with her gratitude. "I couldn't just leave you up there."

"Some men would," she said with certainty.

"You sound bitter."

Was she? Why would that be? she wondered. How could she know with such confidence that Mason Keller was an unusual sort of man? That even though she was alone with him in his dark house, in a gown much too large, she needn't fear him?

"What time is it?"

"Just past midnight. You've been sleeping for seven hours straight. I came in and woke you a few times as Lauren ordered but I don't think you were completely conscious."

"Oh, my. I never meant to sleep so long."

"Sleep's the best thing for you. That's why I let you go back every time you surfaced."

"You don't have to wait up to check on me, no matter what the doctor said. You're not my keeper."

"That's the whole reason you're here rather than stashed away in some hotel, remember? So I can keep an eye on you."

"Surely Dr. Maxwell didn't mean you had to stay up all night long simply to watch over me!"

"Don't worry about it. I was up, anyway."

"I'd always thought farmers went to bed with the sun."

His mouth quirked but he didn't give in to a full-fledged smile. Was he always so solemn, she wondered, or did a sense of humor lurk behind those masculine features?

She likely wouldn't be here long enough to find out.

"First of all," he said, "I'm a rancher, not a farmer. Big difference. And second, I had some business to take care of, anyway. I would have been up whether you were here or not, so it was no big deal to take a break every hour or so to check on you."

"You can see I'm perfectly fine now, right?"

An odd light leaped into those silvery-gray eyes. "Perfectly," he murmured.

For some reason, that single word spoken in a low voice sent shivers skidding down her spine. This would *never* do. She couldn't possibly be attracted to the man. But here in the hush of the night with only the two of them alone in a dimly lit bedroom, she was finding that very difficult to remember.

She cast her mind about for an innocent topic. "I suppose your children are sleeping."

"They'd better be, though putting them down was no easy task. You're the most excitement they've had since the plane ride to the States."

She wondered again about the circumstances that had brought this commanding Utah rancher together with two Filipino children but it seemed impolite to ask.

Perhaps they were his love children.

The thought whispered in her mind, giving her all sorts of inappropriate thoughts. She instantly wondered what kind of lover he would be, with those big hands and that strong, powerful body. Incredible. She didn't doubt it for an instant. He would be the kind of man to make a woman's toes curl and her insides melt into a helpless, quivering mass of need.

Oh, heavens.

She fought the urge to fan her suddenly flaming face and had to hope it was too dark in the room for him to notice.

Where in heaven's name did that line of thought come from? He was a stranger! How could she be entertaining completely inappropriate thoughts about a man she barely knew? Anyway, hadn't Charlie talked about their father and mother being dead?

She searched around frantically for a safe topic of conversation, praying he wouldn't ask about what might have put such color on her cheeks. She settled on the children.

"Charlie and Miriam are charming. I enjoyed their company very much this afternoon with Pam. I hope you don't mind."

He shoved his hands into the pockets of his jeans. "Actually, I've given that some thought this evening and I have to admit, I do mind."

She stared at him, disconcerted, forgetting all about how attractive he might be. "I'm sorry?"

Mason's features looked hard as granite. "I need to ask you to stay away from Miriam and Charlie. I realize that's not an easy task while you're staying in the same house but I have to insist on this."

She lifted her chin, a tangle of hurt and embarrassment lodged in her throat. "I've lost my memory, Mr. Keller. But I have to believe it's not contagious."

A muscle in his jaw hardened. "They're my children now and I'm responsible for their well-being. I won't have them hurt again."

"I would never hurt them!"

"I don't know you from Adam, lady. I've got nothing but your word on that. And the word of a woman who says she has no memory is worth about as much as a pail of hot spit."

Jane wanted to argue with him but she couldn't truly blame him for his caution, his protectiveness toward his children. He *didn't* know her. For that matter, she didn't know herself. Perhaps she was some sort of deranged child killer on the loose.

No. She didn't remember her past but she knew in her heart she could never harm either of those two beautiful children—Charlie with the mischievous light in his eyes and solemn Miriam of the rare, sweet smiles. She would rather climb willingly back into that nightmare permanently than cause them any pain.

She knew she would never hurt them—but she also knew she had no real way to convince Mason Keller of it. And he *was* the children's guardian. She had no choice but to honor his wishes.

"How do you suggest I stay away from them? I suppose I could stay in this room until my memory comes back or your police friend discover my identity."

"You don't have to hide out in here. You're not a prisoner, you're a guest."

"Not a particularly welcome one," she couldn't resist adding.

"I haven't turned you out into the cold, have I?" His words were clipped, abrupt, and instantly filled her with shame.

"No, you haven't. I'm sorry if I seem ungrateful. I'm not."

He sighed. "Look. All I'm asking is that you not encourage the children to form a friendship with you. They've been through enough loss and pain the last few months. They don't need to befriend someone who's leaving in a day or two."

She couldn't find anything unreasonable in a father looking out for his children's best interests, though she anticipated a terribly lonely few days alone here.

"Of course," she murmured. "I'll do my best to be as unfriendly to your children as possible."

"Thank you."

She found the prospect of treating the children with cold civility dismal. It seemed against her nature. In an odd, convoluted way, she found a certain comfort in that. Surely she couldn't be too terrible a person if she found the idea of hurting two innocent children so reprehensible.

"Are you all right now if I leave?" he asked after a pause.

She flushed, embarrassed all over again about that silly nightmare. "Yes. Fine. I'll try not to disturb your sleep anymore tonight."

For some reason she couldn't decipher, he seemed to find that amusing. "I appreciate that," he murmured. "But don't worry about it. I don't sleep much, anyway."

"Too many ghosts?"

Surprise flickered across his features briefly, followed by a quick, raw pain, then both emotions were quickly concealed. "We all have them, I suppose."

Did she? she wondered. Surely she did. Perhaps it was a blessing that she couldn't remember them.

Mason headed for the door. "You can keep the light on all night if you need to."

She wanted to be brave and strong, to tell him to go ahead and turn off the light, that she would be fine. But the idea of lying here in this strange bed in the dark left a hard, cold knot of dread in her stomach. She couldn't do it, no matter how deeply she wanted to.

"Thank you," she murmured, ashamed of her cowardice.

She lay there in that spartan bedroom for a long time after he left, gazing at the light and wondering about those ghosts she couldn't remember and a nightmare she couldn't quite forget.

Two months away from the job and he was turning soft.

More disturbed than he cared to admit by his encounter with his guest, Mason opened the outside door and walked out onto the porch. June nights in the high desert valleys of Utah were cool and intoxicating. In the heavy, oppressive heat of Southeast Asia, he'd forgotten how pleasant it could be to walk outside and smell sage and pine and the spicy climbing roses his mother had planted next to the porch the year before she died.

He inhaled the clean air deep into his lungs then leaned over the porch railing to gaze up at the vast blanket of stars.

The night was alive with noise—the lowing of cattle, the chirping serenade of crickets somewhere near the house, the leaves of the huge poplars rustling in the breeze. From the Forest Service land that bordered the Bittercreek to the east, a lone coyote howled.

The mournful sound sent chills rippling down his spine.

What was wrong with him? He was a trained operative, ruthless and deadly.

For the sake of his country, he had wallowed in filth and slime, had submerged himself in a world of constant danger and deception.

He had been able to maintain his cover under extreme circumstances and through his work had helped bring some of the world's most dangerous and fanatical extremists to justice.

Vicious characters didn't scare him, the ever-present threat of exposure had become just another part of his life.

So how could the low, frightened cries of a woman he didn't know and didn't trust send his insides churning into panic mode?

He had just been starting up the stairs to check on her when he'd heard those first whimpers. He didn't like remembering how he'd taken the stairs three at a time to race to her side, how he had reached for a weapon he wasn't wearing and burst into her bedroom as if he expected to find an entire al-Qaeda cadre inside.

He also didn't like remembering the relief that had flooded him when he'd realized she'd only been dreaming—or the strange warmth in his chest as he watched her battle her night demons.

He should have let her sleep, but he hadn't been able to stand her soft, mewling cries.

It had been all he could do not to pull her into his arms, to hold her close and do his damnedest to keep whatever she feared at bay.

What was it about his mysterious houseguest that affected him so strongly? She was lovely, certainly, with that dark hair and those soft, vulnerable smoky-blue eyes.

And the accent didn't hurt. He couldn't deny he found it an incredibly erotic contrast to stand in the low light of that bedroom and listen to that prim and proper Mary Poppins voice while her loose nightgown gaped open just enough to show him a few tantalizing hints of the curves beneath it.

He closed his eyes, disgusted with himself.

Despite his undeniable attraction, he didn't trust the woman. He *couldn't* trust her. He had more than just himself to look out for now; he had the care of two grieving children who needed him to be ever watchful, always on guard.

How long had it been since he'd been with a woman? he wondered again.

Too damn long, if he could become so aroused by a mysterious stranger with a head injury and a boatload of trouble.

He had never been some kind of James Bond type, with a different woman on his arm every day of the week. But he was a red-blooded male. He enjoyed women and enjoyed sex.

But he had the children to think about now. Even if he could find someone willing, he couldn't just go running around town, scratching any random itch. What kind of example would that set for Charlie and Miriam?

He couldn't forget the hard reality that his life had changed forever the day Samuel and Lianne were killed. His swinging bachelor days were gone now, traded in for SpongeBob cartoons and McDonald's Happy Meals.

This was his life now and he couldn't regret it.

The coyote howled from the mountains again and this time it was joined by another cry farther to the south.

Mason listened to their duet for a moment longer, then turned around and walked back inside to find his solitary bed.

Chapter 6

She awoke to the soft patois of Tagalog coming from the doorway of the bedroom.

Still caught in the hazy world between sleep and consciousness, she listened to the murmurs and caught snatches of low-pitched conversation, mostly giggles from Charlie and solemn responses from his sister.

She couldn't quite bring herself to open her eyes, charmed by these children and their sweet innocence.

The world outside seemed frightening, intrusive. She wanted to stay here in these cozy blankets forever listening to them, safe and at peace, but inevitably the wispy tendrils of sleep began to recede.

With her return to full consciousness, she knew these children were Charlie and Miriam Betran, their adoptive father was a darkly gorgeous man named Mason Keller and they had a talkative but kind housekeeper by the name of Pam Lewis.

But who was *she?*

She dug around in her memory but still came up with nothing.

Oh, she remembered vividly all that had happened the day before, from the moment she'd opened her eyes and found Mason Keller standing over her, to that oddly intimate encounter with him in the hush of midnight.

She had no trouble conjuring up the scent of him, that enticing combination of sandalwood and sage and the way his silver-gray eyes narrowed with suspicion whenever he looked at her.

Like a movie she had seen a dozen times, the events of the day before were crystal-clear in her mind. But anything beyond that moment he had found her was still shrouded in a hazy, ominous darkness.

The comfortable warmth and peace of a moment before gave way to a sharp burst of panic.

She still had no idea who she was, where she had come from, what she was doing here, and the realization terrified her all over again.

Had she ever given much thought to how a person's memories define her? Without memories, she had nothing. She *was* nothing—an empty, aimless husk.

"I think she is awake." Even through her efforts to squash the rising anxiety, Jane had to smile at Charlie's firm, over-loud declaration.

She opened her eyes and discovered he had moved from the doorway into the room and stood by her bed watching her like an entomologist with a particularly interesting specimen.

Miriam still hovered just outside the room, her small features entirely too solemn for such a young girl.

"How did you know I was awake?" Jane asked Charlie in Tagalog.

"When you sleep, you sound like this." Mouth open, he made a tiny snoring sound.

Jane gasped with laughter. "I do not! Do I?"

She looked to Miriam for confirmation. The older girl smiled a little and nodded as she moved into the room.

"Our papa made noise when he slept," Charlie announced. "He sounded like this."

He made a loud, snorting noise rather like an angry bull and Jane couldn't help laughing.

"Oh, dear. I don't believe Mason would appreciate you sharing that information!"

"Not Mr. Mason. Our other papa."

"He is dead." Miriam's resigned voice just about broke Jane's heart. "So is our mama."

Oh, my dears. She wanted to hug them both to her and kiss away the pain in their dark eyes. "You told me yesterday. I am very sorry."

"Mr. Mason is our new papa now," Charlie told her. "He is nice for a new papa but not the same as our old papa. Our old papa told us stories and gave us sweets and tickled us. Mr. Mason does not know the stories. And we don't have a mama at all. Mr. Mason said we don't need one, but Miriam and me we think we do."

She wasn't quite sure how to respond to that. "You have Pam," she pointed out.

Miriam's shrug seemed to discount that observation. "She is nice but she does not live here like a real mama would."

Both gave her expectant looks loaded with meaning and Jane felt a spurt of panic of a completely different sort.

Somehow she doubted Mason would be keen on that idea. Or on this conversation at all, she suddenly remembered. What were his words of the night before?

All I'm asking is that you not encourage the children to form a friendship with you. They've been through enough loss and pain the last few months. They don't need to befriend someone who's leaving in a day or two.

She cast a quick glance toward the door, half-afraid he would come bursting into the room at any moment, guns blazing, and order the children from the room.

"Where is Mr. Mason?" She tried for a nonchalant tone, though she suspected she failed miserably.

"He is gone today," Miriam said. "We are to stay with Pam and out of trouble, he said."

Where? she wondered but couldn't bring herself to ask. His whereabouts were none of her business, she supposed, and it seemed somewhat underhanded to interrogate the children.

She couldn't help her curiosity, though, nor could she deny that she found the man fascinating. He seemed such a study of contrasts—intense, almost dangerous, yet gentle and patient with these wounded children.

There was also something so intriguingly familiar about him. She couldn't escape the sensation that she should know him, though he assured her they hadn't met.

She sat up and was relieved when the room only spun a little.

"You are feeling better?" Miriam asked in English.

"Much better. Thank you."

"I am glad you will not die."

Jane gave the girl a wobbly smile, humbled and immeasurably touched. What a sweetheart this child was.

"I'm glad for that too, *ne ne*." Little sister.

Miriam's smile lit up her thin features, revealing tiny dimples in her cheeks.

"Mama called me *ne ne*," she said softly.

Did Mason know that? Jane wondered. Perhaps she ought to remember to tell him. It might help the girl transition to her new life if she could hear the same endearment her mother used from her new caregiver.

"There you are, you rascals."

Jane looked up at the voice from the doorway. Pam stood there watching them, her hands on her hips and her broad features exasperated. "You know you're not supposed to be in here bothering Jane while she's trying to get some rest!"

The children exchanged guilty looks and both stepped away from the bedside.

"It's all right," Jane said quickly, loathe to see the children in trouble. "I don't mind their company. They're both dears."

"You need to sleep."

"I'm fine, honestly. I can't lie around here all day." To put action to her words, she slid from the bed, hitching her too-big nightgown up her shoulder.

"To be perfectly honest, I was hoping you might put me to work somehow. I don't believe I like this lady-of-leisure business."

Pam looked thoughtful. "I don't know. Mason left orders that you should rest."

He also left orders for her to stay away from his children. She thought of his arguments, that Miriam and Charlie had suffered enough loss, that spending time with her would only lead to more heartbreak for them when she left here.

She couldn't discount his fears. Somehow she thought she had some idea what it was like to lose someone dear to her. But wouldn't they be hurt and feel rejected if she treated them with cold disdain and shunned their company, hiding out here in her room?

Perhaps she could find some middle ground. If she treated them with polite but distant friendliness, they wouldn't be able to grow too attached to her and thus wouldn't suffer when she left.

"Will Mason return soon?"

Pam shook her head. "He and Burnell—my husband, remember?—drove up to Weber County this morning for a cattle auction. They won't be back until tonight."

She ignored the twinge of guilt for what she was about to do. "I can't stay in this room by myself all day, Pam. I could never stand it. I would love to be useful."

Pam appeared to consider. "Well, the children and I have strawberries to pick and then we were going to make some of my famous jam, weren't we, kiddos?"

The children both nodded and Jane realized Mason was right about this, at least—both children appeared to understand far more English than they let on. They seemed to know exactly what Pam had said.

"I love the strawberries," Charlie declared, smacking his lips.

Pam chuckled and tousled his hair. "Don't I know it, mister? We're lucky we have any berries left in the garden with those sticky fingers of yours."

Okay, maybe their English wasn't perfect yet. Idioms appeared beyond Charlie as he gazed at his hands in confusion.

"Making jam sounds lovely. Will you let me help, then?"

Pam made a face. "Don't know why you want to. It's a

sticky, hot business. But I won't turn down another set of hands."

Jane smiled, delighted at the prospect of doing something useful. "I'll just dress then and be down shortly."

The anticipation gathering steam inside her crashed to the ground in an ignoble heap. "Oh, dear. I forgot. I have nothing to wear."

"Not to worry, honey," Pam answered. "I raided my daughter's closet for a couple of outfits since you're such a little thing. The two of you look to be about the same size. I'll leave them on the bed here for you."

"You've been so kind. I can never thank you enough."

"Don't worry about it. You just work on getting your memory back so you can give me all the dirty details of your life. I'll be the hit of my bunco club for months with the inside gossip track."

Jane showered quickly. She combed out her hair but wasn't sure how she usually fixed it so she simply pulled it back into a ponytail then gazed intently at her reflection for some hint of something recognizable.

What an odd feeling, to be staring at a virtual stranger in the mirror—and quite an ordinary one, at that. Her eyes were quite lovely, she had to admit, a deep, dark blue, but the rest of her features were unremarkable. Straight nose, slightly large mouth, pale skin.

After several fruitless moments of gazing at that stranger in the mirror, she gave up and returned to her bedroom, where she found two pairs of blue jeans and several cotton blouses, all in eye-popping colors, folded neatly on the quilt.

Oh, my. She wasn't used to such bright shades.

The thought took her aback. How would she possibly

know that? She wracked her brain trying to remember and suddenly had a clear image of a black suitcase sitting open on a bed in a nondescript hotel room.

The luggage was packed with what looked to be a half-dozen business suits in black and navy blue, all of them classic in cut and style and utterly, completely boring.

Was the suitcase hers? It had to be. Why else would she remember it so clearly and also know without a doubt that she favored conservative suits rather than cropped lime-green T-shirts?

Why couldn't she remember something useful, like where that suitcase might be sitting at this very moment?

If her subconscious was going to send her such a tanta-lizing memory, it ought at least to have the decency to let her get a peek at the luggage tag, she thought, disgruntled.

No, the only thing she could see clearly was that suit-case full of drab clothing lying open on a bed.

Did that mean she was a businesswoman of some sort? Could that be a clue into why she was in the States, if, in-deed, she was British as her accent seemed to indicate? A business trip might make sense, but how had she ended up in the mountains, lying in the middle of the road?

She couldn't come up with any more explanations than she had before that random memory popped into her mind, and she finally sighed.

She ought to at least tell Mason. Perhaps that might help him determine where she had come from and he could check local hotels to see if someone matching her descrip-tion came up missing.

He wasn't here, though, she remembered, and wouldn't be back at his ranch until that evening. She would just have to remember to tell him when he returned, she decided, and studied the youthful-looking clothes on the bed once more.

Perhaps they weren't in her usual style but they looked comfortable enough and it was kind of Pam's daughter to lend them. Anyway, right now she didn't really have a usual style. She wasn't bound by expectations, either her own or from others.

It was a curiously liberating realization. Without a past to tie herself to, she could become whatever kind of person she wanted to be. If she wanted to be young and hip, who would tell her she couldn't?

She pulled on the blue jeans and the T-shirt, then gazed at herself in the mirror above the dresser. She looked like a young university student on holiday.

She tossed her hair back, grinned at that vibrant, fun-looking woman in the mirror, then headed off to make strawberry jam.

Following the sound of voices, she found her way back to the huge farm kitchen where Miriam and Charlie were at the table, nearly bouncing off their chairs with impatience.

"All right, then," she said with a smile. "Let's go pick some strawberries."

"Not so fast, girl."

Pam set down a heaping plate of scrambled eggs, bacon, hash browns and thickly buttered toast. She followed it up with a tall glass of orange juice, then gestured to the table.

"Sit. We're not going anywhere until you eat something."

Jane studied the overloaded plate. "You didn't need to go to so much trouble. Toast and coffee would be fine, honestly. I'm afraid I'm not much for eating breakfast."

Pam raised an eyebrow. "And how would you possibly know that?"

The same way she knew she rarely wore lime green, but for some reason she decided to keep that information to herself.

"Instinct," she murmured.

"Maybe your instincts are wrong," Pam answered. "Anyway, even if they're not, there's no reason you can't change that. In some ways, you're starting all over again."

She thought of that refreshing moment in her bedroom when she'd realized she could become anyone she wanted—for now, at least, until her memory returned.

Pam was right. She *was* hungry and she couldn't think of a single reason why she shouldn't eat a hearty breakfast, simply because she didn't think it was the norm for her.

"Thank you," she said and sat at the wide, scarred table across from the children.

"You're welcome. Dig in, now. It's the best way for your strength to come back."

She did, and was amused to find the children watching her every move as she carefully spread a napkin on her lap, sipped at her juice, then sampled a delicate bite of eggs.

"Delicious," she declared.

Pam smiled her gratitude and went back to cleaning the countertop of toast crumbs.

"Thank you for the clothes, by the way," Jane added. "Please tell your daughter thank you, as well."

"I thought you might be close to Julie's size. She left plenty of things when she went off to college last year. I'm afraid they're a little young in style, mostly Abercrombie & Fitch and Old Navy, but at least you'll have something more your size."

"Will she mind me borrowing them?"

"Oh, heaven's no. Julie's a sweet thing and I'm not saying that just because I'm her mother. I'm sorry you can't meet her but she's working up at Grand Teton National Park in Wyoming during summer break."

"Do you have other children?"

"A boy, Anson. He's in college, too, set to graduate in the fall. Goes to Utah State University up in Logan, ag science. He's been on the dean's list every term since he was a freshman."

"How wonderful!"

"He's a good kid. They both are. Usually Anson comes home to help his dad in the summers on the ranch but he had some credits to finish so he decided to go summer term and wrap things up. Of course, it doesn't hurt that he has a girlfriend up there. I guess she's probably a lot more exciting than the old family ranch."

"Two children in college! That's marvelous."

"Not on the pocketbook, I'll tell you. That's why Burnell agreed to run the Bittercreek after Mason's father died in addition to our place. Mase needed somebody to manage it while he was gone and we needed the extra cash. It worked out for everybody."

Jane wanted to ask where Mason had been but before she had the chance, Charlie heaved a deep sigh and shifted in his seat. The children were both fidgeting impatiently, probably anxious for the grown-up conversation to be done so they all could get to the berries.

Pam must have had a similar thought. "Why don't you two take a couple of those old ice-cream buckets from under the sink and get started out there? We'll join you in a minute."

Charlie nodded vigorously and raced for the sink to find the buckets. A moment later, the children hurried out into the June sunshine, slamming the kitchen door behind them.

After they left, the kitchen seemed unnaturally quiet. Pam shook her head. "Those two are real characters. That Miriam's as sweet as can be but I can tell Charlie's going to be a handful. I hope they're not too much of a bother for you."

Guilt trickled through her. "Mason's asked me to stay away from them," she admitted.

Pam's friendly expression registered surprise. "Why?"

"He doesn't trust me." She pushed a small mound of eggs from one side of her plate to the other, frustrated by the entire situation. "He thinks I might cause them harm somehow. I don't know much about my life before yesterday but I can't believe I would ever hurt a child."

"You'll have to forgive Mason. He's new to the whole fatherhood thing and I'm afraid he's still a little uptight where the kids are concerned."

Jane sipped her coffee. "Though knowing Mason," Pam went on, "I can't say he wouldn't have the same reaction a dozen years from now, after he's had plenty of experience being a father. Mason can be a hard man."

A mild understatement, she thought. The man had a glare that could cut grooves in tungsten. "I had guessed as much. Has he always been this way?"

"I suppose so. He was a tough kid who grew into a tougher man. Not that he had much choice, I suppose. His mama died when he was thirteen or so—the cancer—and both he and his dad took it hard. I was newly married, just moved in over at our place, and I really felt for both of them. They fought all the time and Mason took off as soon as he graduated from high school. He hated this place and couldn't wait to leave."

Pam started to clear her plate but Jane shook her head,

unwilling to let the other woman wait on her further—and hoping she would continue more of this fascinating discourse on Mason Keller.

"Where did he go?" she asked, loading her dishes into the dishwasher.

"Joined the Army. Special Forces. Rangers, I guess. Best thing for him, you ask me. He didn't come back often over the years but the few times he did, I could see the changes in him. Everybody could. Mason went in an angry kid and after only a few months they made a man out of him. It was like watching steel temper in front of my eyes. He just seemed to get harder and harder over the years."

Pam shook her head with a smile. "But not so hard that he couldn't forgive. He and his dad made their peace about five years ago, a couple of years before Boyd Keller died of a heart attack. But even when they were on the outs, I never saw a man so proud of his boy as old Boyd."

Jane returned the other woman's smile, relieved that Mason hadn't had to endure his father's death with regrets or self-recrimination.

Did she have living parents, someone who might be worrying for her? She had a quick flashing image of a handsome, distinguished man with a charming smile and piercing blue eyes. She caught her breath, trying to burn the image into her mind, but she had grabbed hold of it an instant too late. It was gone so quickly she couldn't catch it.

She gave a tiny whimper, though she wasn't really aware of it until Pam reached out and touched her shoulder.

"Are you all right?"

Jane exhaled slowly. "I thought I was grabbing hold of some memory there but it slipped away."

Pam pulled her into a quick hug that Jane had to admit

she found wonderfully comforting. "You poor thing. I can't imagine how frightening this must be for you. But don't you worry. We're going to help you through it and before you know it, you'll be your old self again."

Whatever—or whoever—that was, Jane thought. After her terrifying dreams the night before, she was almost more afraid that her memory *would* come back. And that she wouldn't like what she remembered.

It was nearly 10:00 p.m. when Mason walked into the Bittercreek kitchen. His back ached from lying on gravel for two hours trying to fix the damn fuel pump on Burnell Lewis's truck and he hadn't eaten since wolfing down a charred hamburger at the auction in between bids and that was nine hours ago.

All he wanted was a little food in his stomach and a warm bed. But first he was going to have to be a man and face the wrath of Pam, who had been stuck here for fourteen hours with his kids.

He didn't suppose it would do any good for him to use the excuse that the delay could be firmly blamed on her husband's piece-of-crap truck. Pam wasn't exactly the forgiving sort.

Might as well face his medicine.

"Pam?" he called softly as he walked through the house looking for her. She didn't answer—nor did she come running out wielding a frying pan to bean him with.

Frowning, he headed up the stairs. He opened Charlie's bedroom door and found the room empty, his bed unused. Maybe she'd taken the children over to the Lewis place to sleep—but wouldn't she have left some kind of note if she had so he wouldn't rip the house apart looking for them?

When he walked across the hall to Miriam's room,

though, he found them both asleep on the floor, atop the intricately woven *banig* they had brought from their home.

He shouldn't have been so surprised, Mason thought. Though they had separate bedrooms, more often than not, he found them together in one of their rooms, usually on the *banig*. He supposed in some ways the traditional sleeping mat was a security blanket for them, one of their last ties to the life they'd left behind.

Though it frustrated him that they didn't feel comfortable yet here with him, he couldn't really blame them. This had to be a terrifying time for two young children, uprooted from everything familiar and thrust into a world where they knew no one but him and each other.

Miriam and Charlie had few constants in their world right now and he understood their need to cling to each other—and to the comfort of something that had belonged to their parents.

He understood, but he couldn't help wishing he had some kind of guidebook to help him know when they should be ready to separate a little from each other. At least when they might be comfortable enough in his home to spend the night in their own rooms. How was he supposed to know these kinds of things?

So at least one mystery was solved—he knew where the children were. But where was Pam? He couldn't believe she would just leave them here. He had a good mind to head over to the Rocking L and give her a piece of his mind.

He was still stewing when some subtle change in the atmosphere—a scent, a tiny sound, perhaps just a shifting of molecules—warned him that he was no longer alone.

Instantly alert, he whirled, instinctively reaching for a weapon he wasn't wearing.

Chapter 7

His houseguest.

His hand dropped to his side and he stood in the dim hallway feeling foolish.

She was lovely in the low light, small and ethereal. She wore jeans and a T-shirt in a color that reminded him of key lime pie and had pulled her hair back in a ponytail thing that made her look about sixteen.

Something about seeing her this way struck a chord and he cocked his head, trying to figure out why she looked so familiar.

"I'm sorry," she murmured. "I didn't mean to startle you."

He'd just spent more than a dozen years as a government spook. He refused to allow himself to be startled in his own damn house.

"You didn't," he lied, then he felt even more foolish

when she raised her eyebrows in a doubtful look, as if she knew perfectly well he wasn't telling the truth.

"Where's Pam?" he asked, mostly in an effort to change the subject. "I called for her when I came home but she didn't answer."

"She's not here, I'm afraid. She left around six-thirty."

"Really? The kids were in bed that early?"

She shook her head, peering into the room where Miriam and Charlie were curled up on the floor. "Shall we discuss this downstairs so we don't wake the children?"

Without waiting for an answer, she headed for the stairs and Mason had the distinct impression by the stiffness of her shoulders that she was retreating down the stairs to avoid meeting his gaze.

In the kitchen, she leaned against the counter, her arms folded across her chest. He thought he saw apprehension in smoky-blue eyes but she hid it behind a pleasant smile.

"Pam had a terrible migraine," she said in that prim British accent he was disgusted to discover hadn't lost one bit of its effect on him. "I could see her poor head was throbbing so I encouraged her to go home. The children and I could manage just fine for a few hours. We did. We played a game then read for a while, they took their baths and then they went straight to sleep about an hour ago."

He had just endured one hell of a miserable day, between the cattle auction where he'd felt incredibly out of his depth despite Burnell Lewis's amused tutoring, and then losing the blasted fuel pump on the way home. The whole time he'd been away, he had been worried about the kids and how they were doing without him.

His mood hadn't improved at all when he'd talked to Daniel Galvez a few hours earlier and learned that the sheriff's deputies hadn't found any trace of a car accident in the general area where he had stumbled upon Jane the day before, and he was no closer to discovering who this stranger might be.

A call to Cale Davis revealed the FBI agent had much the same information—zip.

And now to discover the woman in question had not only defied his firm orders to stay away from his children, but had actually spent several hours alone with them, seemed like the final straw.

Mason did his best to rein in his anger. Though he was annoyed with Pam for leaving, he couldn't be *too* angry with her, especially if she was ill. He already owed her more than he could ever repay for all she had done for them since he'd moved back to the Bittercreek with the kids. She had taken them all under her wing and insisted on helping him with the cooking and the kids during the summer until school started.

No, the bulk of his aggravation was directed at this woman, with her big blue eyes and her innocent appearance and her sexy voice that was driving him crazy.

"I seem to remember a conversation last night where I asked you to leave Miriam and Charlie alone."

"You did." She lifted her chin and those smoky eyes were wary but defiant.

He hated that his gut clenched with desire as he watched her. How could it be that even though he was exhausted and annoyed and starving, his body could still respond instantly to this woman he didn't trust?

"I see." Through fierce effort, he was able to keep his voice calm. "So you thought the best way to honor my efforts to protect my children would be to spend the entire evening with them."

Color rose on her high cheekbones but she didn't retreat. "It wasn't just the evening. I suppose you'll find out eventually, as Charlie and Miriam aren't exactly discreet, so I might as well tell you now before you hear it from them in the morning. The truth is, Pam and I and the children spent the entire day together picking strawberries and then preserving them. It was quite lovely, actually. There's fresh strawberry jam in the refrigerator if you'd care for some and Pam made bread this morning."

His stomach growled at the prospect of homemade bread and jam, which only added to his frustration. "No, I wouldn't care for any fresh strawberry jam! What I would like is for somebody in my own home to listen to me once in awhile."

She looked down at the peeling linoleum of the kitchen floor. "I listened to you. I even agreed with most of what you said."

"But you decided what I asked didn't matter, you would just go ahead and do what you wanted anyway."

Her sigh somehow made *him* feel like the guilty one. "I think when my memory returns I'm going to discover I must be a terribly selfish person," she said after a moment.

He frowned, more at the note of self-disgust in her voice than at her words. "Why do you say that?"

"I couldn't bear the idea of spending all day alone in my room, Mason. I *couldn't*. I know what you said last night about wanting to protect your children. I respect you for that, I *do*, and the last thing I would ever wish would be to hurt them."

"They're lonely and frightened and desperate to make attachments wherever they can. Don't you think they'll view it as another loss when you leave?"

Any defiance she might have worn at the beginning of their conversation had trickled away. "I hope not. I had it all worked out in my mind, that I would hurt them more if I ignored them or avoided them. I thought if I could be distantly polite with them, they wouldn't care when I left. But the truth is, I just couldn't bear the thought of spending all day staring at the walls of my room. I would suffocate in that room without someone to talk to."

This whole situation was enough to make him miss the tense intrigue of Mindanao.

He could see it wouldn't have been fair to ask her to hide out in her room. He should have thought this through better, perhaps taken the children with him to the cattle auction so this problem wouldn't have come up. He carried as much blame in this as she did.

"I just don't want to see them hurt more than they have been," he finally said.

"Oh, neither do I, Mason." Her smile was quick and genuine. "They're wonderful children. Sweet and funny and so eager to please. I wanted to be distantly polite with them but I found it just too difficult."

He couldn't help noticing how Jane's features became bright and animated when she talked about the children.

"Miriam is so quiet," she went on, "but I can tell there's so much going on inside that mind of hers. And her eyes! I know she's only nine but have you noticed her eyes are those of an old, wise woman? I think she must know the secrets of the universe. Do you know her mother called her *ne ne?* Little sister? I used the endearment and you should have seen her face light up! You should try it. And Charlie. What a rascal! You know, I think he ate an entire bucket full of strawberries before we could even carry them inside.

He had both Pam and me laughing all afternoon, even with Pam's headache."

Boy, he really must be getting into this whole fatherhood thing if hearing someone praise the children could fill him with such pride.

"Yeah, they're great kids."

Jane lapsed into silence but he could see questions forming in her eyes. Even before she opened her mouth to speak, he steeled himself for what she might ask.

"I know this is terribly forward of me," she said, "but can you tell me how they came to be living here with you? What happened to the children's parents?"

The crushing guilt he had borne for two months reared up as he thought of the long, tragic journey that had led them all here. Samuel, Lianne, the car bombing that had killed them.

He had the oddest urge to tell her about it, to confide his own culpability in their deaths. He opened his mouth to do just that, then shut it with a snap.

He *was* turning soft. Why should he even *consider* confiding in this woman, this stranger? He didn't like the fact that he'd been tempted to break the first unwritten rule of espionage: Keep your mouth shut at all costs.

He knew nothing about her, he reminded himself. Oh, she might seem innocent and genuinely drawn to his children, but it could all be an act to pry information out of him—for whatever purpose, nefarious or otherwise, he couldn't begin to guess.

He pushed away from the kitchen counter. "They're mine now. That's the only thing that matters."

Her color faded a little at his curtness and she drew in a breath. "Of course. I'm sorry for prying. None of this is any of my concern. I *have* no concerns, I suppose, do I? At least until I remember who I am."

How could she make him feel so damn guilty for his shortness? He wasn't sure how she did it, but he found it humiliating that the woman could play him like nobody else. He vowed not to let her get to him, with her softness and her air of fragility.

"I do have concerns. My children. I'm all they have now and I will do whatever it takes to protect them."

"Of course. That's as it should be, Mr. Keller." Her voice was cold, tight, and no trace of softness showed in those smoky-blue eyes now. He told himself he was relieved, that things were easier that way. But somehow he had a hard time believing it.

"Thank you for watching them tonight but in future—"

"I know." She cut him off before he could complete the sentence, grimly certain what he intended to say. "In future, you would prefer I leave Charlie and Miriam alone."

"It can't be that hard. It's only for a few days. Your memory will be back soon and then you'll be out of here, on your way to wherever it is you're supposed to be."

Jane knew she should have been heartened by his comment, that soon things would once more be as they should, but she was aware of a deep sense of unease fluttering low in her stomach.

The thought of what might await when her memory returned left her depressed and rather frightened of the unknown. Still, she decided to put on a brave face. "Right. Absolutely."

Her efforts at sangfroid apparently fell short of complete success. Mason's brow furrowed as he studied her carefully. "What is it? Have you remembered something about your past?"

She thought of the odd flickers of memory that had haunted her all day. First had been that strong image of a suitcase and the boring, bland wardrobe it contained, then the man's face she couldn't quite remember.

Even more disturbing had been not so much a clear memory as an odd, twisting fear that writhed through her at random moments. She and the children had been out in the garden picking berries when it had struck her for the first time.

She had been basking in the jumbled beauty of the overgrown garden, in the June sun warm on her shoulders and plump bees buzzing in the flowers. The garden smelled sweet and musty and the sky had been a stunning blue and she couldn't imagine there could be another place on earth she would rather be than right there.

Lost in enjoying the moment and determined to burn this one into her flawed memory, at least, she had been taken unaware by a cloud drifting past the sun. She wasn't aware of the shift but suddenly the lovely, peaceful garden had turned into somewhere dark and terrifying.

As she'd stared at the sky, she had been struck by the compelling sensation that something important lurked just on the other side of her subconscious, something frightening and ugly. She hadn't *wanted* to remember it, but she couldn't shake the feeling that she *had* to, that something dire would happen to a great many people if she didn't.

What was it? She had to think. She needed to remember so she could *tell* someone....

What? *What* did she need to remember? Try as she might, there in that tangled mess of a garden, she couldn't come up with the answer to that burning question.

The cloud shifted away from the sun and she was once more in a cheery garden spot in Utah with the birds twittering in the treetops and the mountains comforting and solid in the distance.

While she and the children had finished picking the berries, she'd tried to catch hold of what had seemed so important but nothing came to her. And though that anxiousness, that sense of impending evil, had washed over her several more times throughout the afternoon while she and the children helped Pam with the laborious process of making jam, she hadn't come any closer to figuring what it all might possibly mean.

"Did you remember something?" Mason asked again now, his silvery eyes spearing her to the wall of the kitchen with their intensity.

She shivered under the sheer force of that gaze that seemed to see right through her skin. If he ever decided to give up ranching, he could make a living interrogating hostile combatants, she thought.

Pam had said he had been in the Army Rangers. Perhaps that had been his specialty, prying secrets out of the enemy. She wasn't sure she liked that idea.

She did know she certainly couldn't equivocate very well around him. "I didn't remember anything concrete," she admitted. "A few random images, but I can't imagine what they might mean. I saw a suitcase with women's business suits."

Oh, and I'm suffering delusions of grandeur that something locked in my memory bank might be important to the security of the world. But other than that, it's been a slow day.

"I don't suppose you found anything out about me, did you?" she asked him.

"Don't you think I'd tell you if I had?"

"I hope so."

He studied her for a moment, then shook his head.
"Daniel Galvez said his deputies searched all the logging
roads in a two-mile radius from where I found you and
didn't find anything to indicate a car accident."

She sighed, depressed all over again. "I suppose that would
have made everything just too easy, wouldn't it? To find an
automobile with a handbag containing full identification.
Driving license, passport, diplomatic papers, everything."

He stared at her. "What did you say?"

"Sorry?"

"You said diplomatic papers."

She looked at him blankly. "Did I?"

"Yes!"

"Why on earth would I say that?"

"I don't know. Maybe you're somehow attached to the
British consulate, traveling in Utah on diplomatic business.
That might at least give us a place to start."

Hope flickered through her. To know who she was
again, to have a place in the world instead of all this frustrating blankness, seemed within her reach once more.

Nibbling at the edges of her hope, though, was more of
that strange anxiety. Some odd, inexplicable instinct
warned her she was better off keeping a low profile here
at the ranch, where no one could find her. She shivered but
to her relief Mason didn't appear to notice.

"I'll call Cale in the morning to tell him what you've remembered and see if that helps narrow down the possibilities," he said. "Maybe by this time tomorrow you'll be
back where you belong."

The thought should fill her with relief, she thought. So
why did she feel this deep sense of loss?

She countered it by manufacturing a smile for Mason. "That would be wonderful. Thank you so much for everything you've done."

"I haven't done anything yet."

"You've opened your home to me, a complete stranger. I can't imagine many people would have done that."

He looked uncomfortable. "Daniel and Lauren didn't give me much choice in the matter."

"You had a choice. You could have said no and made the sheriff take me to some shelter somewhere. I'm very grateful you didn't."

This time her smile was genuine. She meant only to thank him for his help but at her smile, his gaze seemed to lock on to her mouth like a heat-seeking missile and she suddenly realized how alone they were in this darkened house.

The warm intimacy of the evening wrapped around them again, binding them close, and her stomach started a long, slow tremble.

She was suddenly intensely aware of him—of his silvery eyes, vivid and intense, of his rugged features that seemed so oddly familiar, of the smell of leather and horses and male that clung to him.

The air left her lungs in a rush and she could only stare at him, a sudden fierce attraction fluttering through her. He was a remarkably good-looking man, with those distinctive eyes, those rippling, powerful muscles in his chest and shoulders, that overwhelming masculinity.

She wanted him to kiss her, she realized. With a deep, urgent ache, she wanted to lean into him, to wrap her arms around those shoulders and hang on tightly until the rest of the frightening, uncertain world faded into nothingness.

Something kindled in those eyes, something hot and dark, and she recognized some of the same awareness there that she suddenly couldn't seem to breathe around.

He stepped forward and she held her breath, her lips parted and her heart pulsing with anticipation....

At the last instant, just before he would have kissed her, the refrigerator motor rumbled to life and Mason jerked as if he had received an electric shock from it.

In a cold rush, reality intruded and Jane let out her breath, horrified with her instant response to him.

What on earth was wrong with her? She didn't even know the man. Worse, she didn't even know *herself.* What if she had a husband or a boyfriend tucked away somewhere or, heaven forbid, children! She had absolutely no business even *thinking* about kissing Mason Keller, no matter how attractive she might find the man, until her memory returned.

She had to get out of here, to retreat to the safety and solitude of her bedroom. She started to speak then stopped, appalled when her voice came out low and throaty like some kind of West End party girl.

She cleared her throat and tried again. "I... Good night. It's late and I imagine you're more than ready for bed."

A muscle twitched in his jaw. "Right. Bed. It's been a long day and we both could use some sleep."

She couldn't seem to wrench her gaze away from his mouth that had been just a hair's breadth from kissing her, and her stomach whirled as if she'd just stepped off a high-speed lift.

Oh, heavens. She needed to get out of here before she did something idiotic like grab the man and plant one on him.

She murmured another good-night, flashed a hesitant smile, then headed for the stairs.

Chapter 8

Jane woke the next morning to brilliant sunshine streaming in through her bedroom window and an echoing silence that left her restless and edgy.

Her inquisitive little alarm clocks of the day before seemed nowhere in evidence. Perhaps Mason had read his children the riot act and warned them not to disturb her.

This time they must have decided to obey him, she thought. Funny how the sunshine didn't seem as cheerful and bright without the children there smiling and giggling.

No matter. It was better this way. If they weren't here, she wouldn't have to treat them with the cool disdain their father requested. Now if only she could avoid them all day. She supposed she would have to stay in her room after all, though the prospect appealed to her about as much as nibbling a mouthful of broken glass.

With great creativity and effort, she dragged out the

time it took her to shower and dress in more of the young-looking clothes belonging to Pam's daughter. This time she chose a pumpkin orange T-shirt and denims that ended about four inches south of her navel. Though the shirt was long enough to cover her abdomen, she still felt exposed in the hiphuggers.

She wouldn't have dared to wear these kind of clothes if they had been in style when she'd been a teenager. Her father would have pitched a screaming fit. She smiled at the thought, then her smile froze.

Her *father!* She had a father. She must or she wouldn't be so certain of his displeased reaction if he ever saw her wearing a piece of clothing so revealing.

Her father. Was he the man she had remembered so briefly the day before?

What was he like? Was he worried about her? She wanted desperately to remember. Her heart pounding, she scrunched up her eyes and focused as hard as she could, trying to conjure up a face, a smile, anything.

Finally, her head aching and whirling a little from the effort, she opened her eyes and released a heavy sigh. Nothing. She couldn't grab hold of one single memory of the man, couldn't even say for sure whether she'd imagined him in her desperation for some link to her past.

What now? She sighed, flopping back onto the bed-spread. The day stretched out ahead of her, frustrating and dull. If only she could go out in search of Pam, just for companionship of some kind, but the children were likely with her. She couldn't take that chance—she knew she owed it to Mason to try harder to honor his wishes.

She could use some coffee, but going in search of it would also probably lead her to the children.

Anyway, as prisons go, this one was probably more comfortable than most.

She closed her eyes and behind her eyelids flashed an image of a hole in the ground covered with a piece of wavy green metal roofing material.

Dark. Fear. Cold.

Let me out. Oh, please. I want to go home.

Daddy, help me!

Jane blinked back to reality and was once more in Mason Keller's sparse guest bedroom, with its wobbly bedside table and the squat, ugly bureau with the missing knob.

Where had that come from? She shivered, chilled even though the room was a comfortable temperature and likely to get much warmer as the June day wore on.

That couldn't have been a memory. Who has memories like that? Perhaps it was something she'd seen at the cinema or read in a book. She sat up. Still, she couldn't completely discount it. Not when her insides still twitched with a strange mixture of terror and guilt and when she could still smell damp, musty earth and the smell of her own fear.

She needed to write all these impressions down. With what? She opened the small drawer of the bedside table and pawed through the meager contents until she found a stubby, gnawed pencil and a piece of paper.

If she wrote down everything that entered her mind, perhaps she could determine some sort of pattern.

She wrote every impression she could think of about that odd image. Metal scraping, scratchy rope, choking down thick water and a tiny portion of plain rice.

How were they all connected? And did it have anything to do with those eerie moments in the garden the day before? She had no idea but she wrote them anyway, circling them and connecting with lines to the word *suitcase* and *father*.

This all seemed an exercise in futility. The doctor had said she was probably in her mid- to late-twenties. More than two decades of life and all she had were a handful of memories to show for it, and odd ones at that. What if her memory never came back? What if she had to spend the rest of her life never knowing what had come before, what people she might have left behind, who might be looking for her?

Tears burned her eyes and panic fluttered just around the edges of her mind. What if she was trapped in this nothingness forever?

She had to get out of this room. She would go crazy if she had to be shut up here all day with only a few pitiful memories. Perhaps if she went outside, took a way around the ranch, she could still avoid the children.

Working hard to tamp down the rising panic attack, she hurried to the door and yanked it open, only to find Pam on the other side, her arm upraised in a fist, ready to knock.

Jane didn't believe she could ever be so glad to see another human being.

Pam frowned and dropped her hand. "Here, now, what's the matter? You're pale as a ghost. Have you remembered something?"

Oh, she was heartily sick of that question. "Nothing significant." Frustration sharpened her voice. "Just stupid bloody details that don't make any sense."

"I'm sorry, honey. This is so hard on you. But remember, it's only been a few days."

The other woman's calm good sense helped steady her. "I know," Jane answered. "I'm just tired of being a burden."

"You're not a burden. You're a guest. And speaking of such, I thought I heard you moving around up here and wondered if I could interest you in some breakfast."

Her stomach rumbled again and she had an almost violent urge for coffee. "Breakfast would be wonderful. Thank you."

"Why don't you come into the kitchen and keep me company while I scramble some eggs for you?"

Oh, how she would love to sit in that warm, cheerful kitchen. But what if the children were there? The prospect of shunning them filled her with dismay but she couldn't risk angering Mason again. "You know, on second thought, I'm not really hungry after all. I believe I'll just stay here."

Pam cocked her head, green eyes suddenly cool. "I can bring you a tray if you don't feel like a visit."

Oh, dear. Now she'd offended the woman who felt very much like her only friend in the world. "I love talking with you! You've been wonderfully kind. It's just that Mason…"

She faltered, not sure how to finish her sentence without appearing to criticize the man.

"What?"

"He was angry about yesterday," she finally said. "He's asked me again to do my best to discourage the children from forming an attachment to me. I thought it would be better if I avoided them altogether."

Pam shook her head, warm and friendly once more. "You don't have to worry about that this morning, since he took the little rugrats with him for the day. It's just us girls."

Jane sighed with relief, feeling a bit like a hostage finding unexpected freedom.

What an odd way to phrase it, even in her own mind,

she thought. Taken in concert with her odd flash of memory about that hole in the ground and the fear still gnawing in her stomach, she had to wonder what it might mean.

All this worry over something she couldn't explain would make her ill. She vowed to pack it all away for now and focus on the present instead of a past she couldn't pin down.

"I'll come with you on one condition," she said.

Pam raised an eyebrow. "And what's that?"

"That you find something for me to do again today. I have a feeling I'm one who needs to stay busy."

The other woman laughed. "Darlin', you've had the great good fortune to lose your memory in exactly the right place, then. There's always plenty to do at the Bittercreek. This place has been empty for two years. My Burnell has done a good job with the cattle side but the house is falling down around our ears. We picked all the strawberries yesterday but I'm sure I can find something else to keep you busy."

He had spent most of his adult life about as far away from the Bittercreek as he could get, but Mason was surprised how quickly he had eased back into the familiar rhythm of a working ranch.

Several things about returning to his roots took him unawares. He hadn't expected to feel this connection to the ranch that had been in his family for four generations, this deep flare of pride when he looked at what his father and his father's father had built, the even deeper sense of responsibility when he realized the legacy left for him to uphold.

Who would have thought Mason Keller would ever find himself running the Bittercreek? *He* wouldn't have, certainly.

He had left the ranch an angry kid, vowing never to return after that last bitter fight with his father. Both of them had said things they shouldn't have, had channeled years of disappointment into words that stung like a whole nest of stirred-up yellow jackets.

He had hated ranch life—the constant work for such paltry rewards, living on a financial knife's edge, doing the same thing day after endless day until you couldn't tell yesterday from six months ago except by whether you were sweltering or freezing your ass off.

Boyd Keller had thrived on running the ranch. He had *been* the ranch. Maybe that's why Mason had always viewed it with such conflicted emotions—because his relationship with his father had been complicated and tense. Maybe that was also the reason why over the years his animosity toward the Bittercreek had begun to fade as he and his father had worked their way slowly toward peace.

After his father died and left the ranch to him, somehow Mason's views toward it had undergone a subtle but powerful shift. Hip-deep in intrigue and secrecy, deceptions and subterfuge, he had needed something good and decent to hang his dreams on. Without even realizing it, he had started to envision what he could do here.

The Bittercreek had always been a cattle operation, but for the last few years, Mason had started to dream of changing that.

Now, as he drove back to the ranch that had begun to feel like home again, he glanced at the white horse trailer that filled the rearview mirror. He had just written a pretty sizable check on those future dreams. He just had to hope his gamble would pay off.

While Mason didn't foresee a time cattle wouldn't be

part of the ranch, what he really wanted was to breed and train horses. When he'd been a kid, he had loved working with the ranch horses. He'd even ridden one of the cutters he'd trained himself in the national high school rodeo finals.

Though just about every other good and decent thing had been pounded out of him over the last decade, that spark still flickered and danced inside him.

He didn't know if he could do it, but he sure as hell was going to try. Raising horses seemed so clean and straightforward. Honorable. If he succeeded, he would have something decent and good he could leave to Charlie and Miriam.

He glanced across the truck cab at the two of them. Charlie was asleep, his head cushioned on Mason's folded denim jacket. Miriam sat beside him, her hands folded in her lap and her eyes gazing straight ahead.

How was he supposed to reach past that unnatural poise of hers to the grieving child within? he wondered.

"So do you think we made a good buy today?"

She seemed surprised he would ask her opinion and just gazed at him in confusion until he gestured over his shoulder toward the horse trailer.

"Unforgettable back there. What do you think of him?"

She tilted her head, considering. "He is very pretty," she finally said with all the seriousness of an oracle making a solemn pronouncement.

He had to smile. The horse was from champion cutting stock, with a sire who'd won the PRCA finals. *Pretty* didn't begin to cover it. "I hope the ladies think so."

"The lady horses, you mean?"

"Yeah. That's right." He tried to come up with the Tagalog word but his command of the language was far from fluent. Maybe Jane would know, he thought, then was annoyed with himself for thinking of her yet again when he'd vowed to put her from his mind.

"*Mare* is the English word for lady horse."

She repeated it with the same solemn care she gave everything, from setting silverware on the table at dinner time to picking out a candy bar at the grocery store.

He so wanted her to be spontaneous and fun, to enjoy life. He had really heartbreaking memories of seeing her with her mother and father back in the Philippines. Samuel had done his best to keep his children separate from his clandestine dealings with Mason, but he had bumped into the family once at the market.

Miriam had been a little shy at first around a tall American stranger, but she had warmed up enough to give him a smile. Before they parted company, she'd been giggling and laughing like any other nine-year-old girl.

She didn't laugh anymore. Her childhood was one more casualty of the car bombing that had killed Samuel and Lianne.

Mason sighed, thinking how far he had to go to help these children. Every time he thought they were making progress toward normalcy, reality slapped him hard in the face.

Today had been a classic example. Trent Saunders, the man he'd bought the stud from, had a daughter close to Miriam's age. Mason had hoped when he saw the other girl trailing Saunders to the barn that Miriam might find a new friend in her.

Maybe if Miriam could spend a little time around someone her own age, she might remember to relax and smile a bit and maybe even learn to laugh again.

But Miriam had only clutched Charlie's hand tighter,

gazing at the other girl out of those wise eyes of hers until Becca Saunders gave up and wandered away.

"Becca seemed nice," he said now, striving for optimism. "Maybe we could have her over sometime."

Miriam frowned. "Have her over what?"

"Over to the ranch."

"Why?" She looked genuinely confused.

"To hang out. You know. Spend a little time together. You could play dolls or fix your hair or listen to music or whatever girls your age do."

She didn't say anything, only gave him that solemn look, and he wondered if any man had ever been less prepared to parent a nine-year-old girl than he was.

He turned his attention back to the road. He sucked at this whole parenting thing. What was he thinking even to consider bringing two orphans home with him? What the hell did he know about little girls *or* little boys, other than he'd been one of the latter decades ago?

Nothing in his life had prepared him for how tough and unrelenting this was.

He hadn't had a choice, he reminded himself. Samuel had been an orphan himself and Lianne's family—wealthy factory owners in the Luzon region—had disowned her after her marriage to him.

With no extended family to take Charlie and Miriam, Mason had known their future would be a grim one, shoved into some overcrowded, less-than-clean Philippine orphanage until they were considered old enough to fend for themselves.

He couldn't let that happen.

Samuel and Lianne had given their lives for what they believed. The least he could do was give their children the best possible future, the kind of future their parents had dreamed of for them, in a world made a little better, a little more safe through their efforts.

He supported the idea in concept—hell, hadn't he thrown his career to the dogs and spent weeks greasing the palm of every two-bit bureaucrat he could find to bring the kids to the States?—but the reality of fatherhood was a brutal kick in the teeth.

They would work their way through, he reminded himself. They had to. He refused to consider any other alternative. These kids needed a home and in some obscure way he was only just beginning to recognize, he was the one who needed to give it to them.

Charlie woke as they drove up the gravel driveway toward the ranch house.

"We are home already?" he asked sleepily.

Mason tried to take heart from the boy's rather disoriented question. At least Charlie considered the ranch home, even if Miriam still hadn't unpacked her suitcase.

"Time flies when you're having good dreams, right?"

Charlie giggled. "I dreamed of a tiny horse in my pocket," he said in Tagalog. "I took it to the ice-cream store and it stood on the table and ate from my cone and then we went to the park and I pushed him down the slide."

Mason thought about telling him to speak English but decided it wasn't worth interrupting the dream narrative.

"What color was the horse?" he asked instead.

Charlie giggled again. "Purple with white spots. He could talk and I called him *Kabayo*."

Horse in Tagalog. Mason grinned as Charlie chattered

for the remaining half-mile with more adventures he and his pocket pony named Kabayo had together.

"Excuse me," Miriam interrupted them in English as they drove past the ranch house on the way to the barn to drop off the new stud. "Is that not Jane on your ladder? Do you think she is needing help?"

He followed the direction of the girl's pointing finger and only managed to swallow a particularly vile curse at the last minute when he caught sight of Charlie watching, his big eyes curious. The kid soaked up every word like he was Sponge-Bob himself. Mason could just imagine how Pam would strip his ears if she heard Charlie repeating his raw epithet.

Mason's hands clenched on the steering wheel. What was the woman up to now?

Two days after sustaining a serious head injury, she tee-tered on the second-to-the-top rung of his father's rickety eighteen-foot ladder, her hand outstretched as she scrubbed years of grime from one of the second-floor windows.

He had an instant vivid mental image of watching help-lessly while she overextended her reach and tumbled to the ground. With his luck, she would break both of her legs and he would be saddled with those big blue eyes and that sexy British voice for the next six months or more.

The woman needed a damn keeper—and not a burned-out ex-spy with two kids to take care of already.

With his heart in his throat and frustrated anger burn-ing a hole in his gut, Mason shoved the truck into Park and ordered the kids to stay put, even though he knew perfectly well they would ignore him.

Mad at the world, he stalked over to her.

"Get down from there," he snapped harshly. "What the hell were you thinking?"

His heart seemed to sink from his throat to his stomach when she jerked in surprise.

In a grim instant replay of his vivid image of a few moments before, one foot slipped off the rung and she teetered eighteen feet up in the air, scrambling wildly for purchase.

Chapter 9

Jane dug the nails of one hand into the window frame to keep her balance while she clung tightly to the ladder with the other.

Adrenaline spurted through her as she looked down at Mason glowering up at her. He looked dark and dangerous, a furious archangel in a dusty black cowboy hat.

As she studied him, she couldn't help wondering if she might be safer staying here atop this rickety ladder than taking her chances with him down on the ground.

No. She drew back her shoulders. She wasn't about to let some arrogant cowpoke with a white-knight complex intimidate her.

Her knuckles cracked as she released her hold on the window frame. She tried for a casual wave but she was very much afraid it came out more like a peculiar five-fingered spasm.

"Hello," she called down in what she hoped was a chipper tone.

Mason continued to glower at her. "Get down from there before you break your fool neck."

"I'm almost finished. I just have one more corner to do here."

"You're not a maid," he snapped. "Get down. Now."

"I've already sprayed it with cleaner, I only have to wipe it dry now. It would be foolish to leave it when I'm this close to being done."

She put action to words and reached as high as she could to the top right corner of the grimy window, trying to ignore the little clutch in her stomach as the ladder seemed to sway.

"Come on, Jane. Move it."

She defied him only for the thirty seconds it took to finish the job then she climbed down the ladder with slow deliberation. He grabbed her and bodily lifted her off the last few rungs to the ground, then turned her around to face him.

"What were you thinking?" he asked, giving her a little shake. "You're two days off a head injury and here you are climbing an eighteen-foot ladder that was ancient and wobbly twenty years ago. That bump on your head must have rattled your brain more than I thought."

She frowned, annoyed at his tone even as she admitted tiny tremors radiated from her arms where he held her.

"I was simply trying to help. Pam had a great deal to do today and I was doing nothing so I thought to absorb some of her load."

He made a face and released her. "Fine. You could always do a little dusting inside or wash the dishes. You certainly don't need to be up on some eighteen-foot ladder washing my dirty windows. Somehow I don't think that's exactly what Lauren had in mind when she suggested you take it easy for a few days."

"I didn't start out on the ladder. I was to do the ground-floor windows but once I finished them, I decided, why stop there? Anyway, I don't see why I shouldn't be up on a ladder. I feel fine. Great, actually."

Except for the butterflies zinging through her whenever he touched her, but she decided perhaps she ought not to mention that little detail.

He studied her closely, until those butterflies started flitting like mad under that silver-eyed scrutiny. "Any memories come flooding back while we were gone?" he asked.

"None, I'm afraid. My rattled brain is still as empty as a village pub on Sunday morning."

He raised an eyebrow. "I figured that part out the moment I saw you up on that ladder."

His wry tone surprised a laugh out of her and she lifted smiling eyes to his. As soon as she did, her laugh died abruptly. Something about his expression sent those butterflies into manic paroxysms.

She swallowed, aware of a low heat uncoiling inside her. Their gazes held for several seconds and she noted that he looked as unnerved as she felt by the sudden tension buzzing between them.

Before she could think of what to say, the children jumped from the truck with a slamming of doors and hurried over to them.

"Jane! Jane! Guess what? Guess what?" Charlie tugged on her jeans, his funny little face alight with excitement.

She couldn't help smiling, totally charmed by these sweet children. "Hmm. Let me think. Ah, I have it. You brought back an elephant in your caravan there and you're set to name him Frederick?"

Charlie giggled and even Miriam hid a small smile behind her graceful hand.

"No, silly!" Charlie said, still in clear English, she was thrilled to notice. "No elephants live in America."

He frowned, then turned to Mason for confirmation. "Is that not right?"

"There aren't any elephants running wild, maybe, but you can find some in zoos and circuses." Mason repeated the latter few words in Tagalog when Charlie looked confused.

"If not elephants, what do you have in there?" Jane asked.

"A horse. A big one," Miriam answered, her eyes wide and her usually solemn features lit up like it was Christmas morning.

Jane smiled at her. "Is he now? What's his name?"

"Unforgettable. He's a stud and very pretty. We are hoping the lady horses will like him, right, Mason?"

Jane shifted her gaze to him and found him looking rather stunned by Miriam's excitement.

He cleared his throat and ran a big hand over the girl's hair in a tender gesture that made Jane feel absurdly like weeping.

"Exactly," he murmured.

"I'm sure he'll make all the lady horses swoon." Through the emotion in her throat, Jane smiled at Miriam, then suddenly remembered she was to discourage their friendship. During the delightful day spent visiting with Pam and helping her clean, she'd forgotten.

Though it broke her heart, she forced her features into a cool expression. "I suppose I'd best put the ladder away and let you get on, then."

She turned away to do just that but Mason's outstretched arm stopped her.

"I can get the ladder later," he said, his voice slightly gruff. "Why don't you come down to the barn with us and help us unload him and show him around his new place?"

Jane turned, stunned by his words and sensing the offer was more than just an invitation to see the new stud. He was actually encouraging her to spend more time with his children.

Where was this coming from? she wondered, but she decided not to question him. Better just to enjoy the unexpected opportunity.

"Yes! Absolutely."

She left her rag and window cleaner by the ladder and climbed into the truck with the three of them for the ride down to the horse barn, perhaps a hundred yards from the house.

"What kind of horse is Unforgettable?" she asked on the way.

"American quarter horse, champion cutting stock. I'd like to set up a breeding and training operation with him."

At the barn, Mason backed the horse trailer until it butted against a chute. He instructed her and the children to stand out of the way by the railing of a paddock—corral, he called it—while he unloaded the horse from the trailer.

A moment later, he opened the door of the horse trailer and led out a beautiful buckskin stallion with black points and a saucy saunter. The animal whinnied, then stretched and trotted around the corral, obviously glad to be free of his metal confines.

She leaned on the railing, her heart beating a little faster at the sight of such a magnificent animal. Mason stood some distance away inside the paddock, letting the horse become familiar with his scent and his presence, and her attention shifted to him.

The afternoon sun shone warm and appealing, gilding both man and beast, and Jane couldn't seem to look away.

"Is he not pretty?" Miriam asked.

Jane swallowed, her eyes never leaving Mason. "Oh, indeed," she murmured. "Absolutely gorgeous."

Heat soaked her cheeks as soon as she heard her own words and she could only be supremely grateful the young girl likely wouldn't understand the reason for it, even if she should happen to notice Jane's heightened color and slightly uneven breathing.

The horse cantered around the paddock for a few moments. As he explored his surroundings, he stretched long, elegant legs, tossing his dark mane like a teenager in a rock-and-roll band, she thought with amusement.

Soon he extended his curiousity to his audience. He moved in their direction, nostrils flaring as he sniffed them. The children squealed a little and stepped back from the fence but Jane stood her ground, delighted with the magnificent animal.

"You are a handsome devil, aren't you?" she crooned, reaching out to pat neck and withers the color of sun-warmed caramel. "You're full of sauce and ready to run."

The horse whickered as if in agreement, and Jane laughed and patted him again before he cantered away.

"You've been around horses."

She shifted her attention from the horse to Mason, who stood watching her with a narrowed gaze and a considering look in his eyes.

She laughed a little at his confidence. "How would you possibly know that?"

"You weren't afraid of him."

"Why would I be? Oh, he's got plenty of energy but he seems friendly enough."

"Most people who haven't been around horses much tend to be intimidated at first by their size and unpredictability. You reached right out to greet him."

Touching the horse had seemed natural, instinctive, she thought. Like patting a dog or stroking a kitten. She wasn't sure why but she would take Mason's word for it that she had experience.

"We can know for sure."

"How?" she asked warily.

"We can put you up on a horse, see how you go. It might help unlock some of those memories in your brain."

Jane eyed the stallion, still trotting across the corral, mane and tail flying. He looked awfully big all of a sudden. "I don't know..."

"I've got a mare who's pretty gentle. I picked her up last week so I could try to get the kids in the saddle. Maybe if they see you giving it a go, they won't be so nervous around her. You game?"

She couldn't back down now. She swallowed, avoiding another peek at the large animal in the corral. "Certainly."

She had to think it would be worth breaking her neck in exchange for basking in that precious light of approval in Mason's eye for a while.

"Let me just stable Unforgettable here so he doesn't stir things up and then I'll bring out the mare," he said.

All too soon, Mason returned leading a small saddled chestnut mare with a gentle gait and friendly eyes.

Wonderful choice for the children, was her first

thought. She paused at the absurdity of that. How would she possibly know what kind of horse Miriam and Charlie should have?

Still, she took it as a good sign that her subconscious—that nasty customer who no doubt remembered all kinds of things it had decided to keep from her—deemed this horse appropriate for children.

Though Jane sensed her borrowed runners weren't quite the thing for riding, Mason assured her she'd be fine for a few moments. He helped her into the saddle, where she rocked to and fro, trying to settle in.

"Everything okay?" he asked.

She frowned. "It feels familiar but wrong somehow. I know that doesn't make any sense."

He adjusted a stirrup, hovering entirely too near her leg for her personal comfort. "It's probably the saddle. You could be used to an English saddle instead of the Western one. Try to imagine it without the high horn in front and with a lower cantle in the back."

She closed her eyes for a moment and concentrated on the changes he suggested. It *did* seem as if it would be more natural the way he described. She decided to experiment with what she had. She held the reins loosely in her hand, straightened her spine and nudged the little mare forward with her knees.

The horse instantly responded and soon they were walking, trotting, cantering and even galloping around the corral.

After a few stiff moments, she laughed out loud. Mason had to be right. This seemed familiar—wonderfully, joyously familiar. She wanted to ride forever. Still, her muscles seemed stiff and a bit awkward in the saddle and she wondered if perhaps she hadn't ridden for a while.

Oh, for her memory to return so she would be able to answer these simple questions, even in her own mind!

Though she longed to leap the fence and see how fast the mare could take her, she had to be content with riding around the paddock until she thought the children must be growing bored. She reined the horse to a stop in front of the three of them.

"That was wonderful! Thank you. Miriam, Charlie, you need to have a go-round!"

"I will ride the horse now," Charlie said.

"Why don't I put you both up and lead you around the corral a few times?" Mason said. "You can hold on to each other."

Jane gave the girl a reassuring smile and then started to dismount to allow them a turn. Before she could jump the last few feet to the ground, Mason stepped forward and lifted her the remainder of the way.

Her startled gaze flew to his and she found him watching her, his silver eyes gleaming in the afternoon sunlight with an unreadable expression that left her feeling as if she'd just taken a hard tumble.

She couldn't seem to breathe as his wide, powerful hands stayed in place just beneath her ribcage for several seconds longer than strictly necessary. She fought a shiver as her body seemed to sigh with delight at his touch. She wanted more. She wanted him to pull her into those strong arms and hold her close, to press his mouth to hers...

"We ride! We ride!" Charlie exclaimed.

At the boy's voice, Mason released her so quickly she almost wobbled, then he turned to lift Miriam up in her place.

Jane backed against the corral railing, fighting the urge to press her hands to her hot cheeks.

Good heavens! What on earth was the matter with her? Bad enough that she'd lost her memory, now she appeared well on her way to throwing off what was left of her sanity.

She could only be grateful for Charlie's impatience to make them both come to their senses.

Or so she told herself, anyway.

Mason stood in his darkened great room watching raindrops drizzle down the windows.

In Utah, as opposed to the tropical humidity of the Philippines, a good soaker of a summer rain was a rare and precious thing. He knew this was priceless to the ranchers and farmers around here; it was one less time they would have to irrigate thirsty crops, but he still couldn't help resenting it.

The storm left him restless, unable to settle. It was nearly 1:00 a.m. Though he was tired from a long day of physical exertion and fully expected another one the next day, he knew himself well enough to realize that trying to sleep would be an exercise in futility.

He had tried to read for a while but the book hadn't held his attention. From there, he'd started to wander around the house like some kind of wild animal searching for something he couldn't find.

As soon as he realized it, he had forced himself to stop and was now using all his willpower to stay in one place and stare out at the confounded rain.

Who was he trying to fool? He sighed. It wasn't the rain leaving him so itchy and uncomfortable.

The reason was asleep in his guest room upstairs—and he was doing his level best not to picture her up there, that dark hair spread out on the pillow and her lovely, delicate features relaxed and warm.

He couldn't remember the last time he had wanted a woman with such a fierce, hungry need until he could think of little else. How could his body burn for her with this urgent desire when his mind still had so many unanswered questions?

He had to admit, he was having a tough time hanging on to his suspicions about her, though he was still trying his best. She seemed too fragile, too lost for him to go on thinking with any confidence that the whole amnesia thing was an act.

He wanted to believe her.

If he should find anything unsettling, it ought to be that realization. How lowering to discover he wanted to throw a dozen years in counterintelligence out the window and believe the word of a woman who appeared to have dropped out of the sky.

He was thinking with his gonads, not his head. He knew it but he was struck by the memory of her riding the little mare he'd bought for the children, of her stunned delight as she had trotted around the corral that afternoon.

Her eyes had glowed and she hadn't stopped smiling, like a child discovering an old toy, long-forgotten but still very beloved.

As he had helped her from the horse, he hadn't been able to keep his hands off her. If the kids hadn't been there with them, he would have dragged her against the wood corral railing and kissed her until neither of them could move.

Hell, he had been perilously close to doing that, anyway, even with the kids looking on with dark, curious eyes.

He couldn't shake the feeling they were on the cusp of something—either she would regain her memory soon or someone would come forward and file a missing person's report.

To his self-contempt, he wanted it to be the former. He wasn't sure he could handle finding out she had a boyfriend or husband out there looking for her.

Lightning flashed in the distance suddenly and a second later the lamp flickered out for an instant, then flashed back on.

The strike must have hit the power grid somewhere, he thought. Better prepare for an outage in case the next one hit closer and knocked out the grid for longer than an instant.

Relieved to have something to do, he walked through the silent house in search of a flashlight.

He dug through his dad's old junk drawer in the kitchen, through scissors and rubber bands and assorted tools until his hand closed around a heavy Maglite he thought he remembered sending Boyd one year for Father's Day.

He heard the cry just as he was closing the drawer again.

The sound rose from upstairs, a low, frightened moan that spiked the hairs on the back of his neck and sent his body into full-alert status.

One of the kids or Jane? He raced up the stairs two at a time, still clutching the flashlight. At the top, he heard it again, louder this time, a sound of complete terror.

With a grim sense of inevitability, he realized it emanated from Jane's room. He couldn't escape her, he thought. No matter what he did, how hard he tried, he couldn't stay away.

He didn't bother to knock, just pushed open the door. She must have left a small lamp on by the bed when she went to sleep, as she had the night before. What terrors lurked in the dark for her?

In the small, low circle of light he could see Jane huddled beneath the quilt. She slept curled into a ball, in the age-old position of self-protection, but even from the doorway he could see the tiny tremors that shook her slender frame.

She moaned a little and Mason hovered in the doorway, unsure what to do. Should he wake her or let the dream work itself out? He didn't know. He hated thinking of her being afraid, even in a nightmare, but maybe her subconscious would give away a clue or two he could use to uncover her identity.

She slept quietly for a moment or two more. He might have thought the nightmare had left her if not for her rapid, panicked breathing.

"Hurry! They're coming," she cried suddenly. "Oh, please. Daddy! Hurry. *No!*"

Okay, that was enough. He couldn't stand this. He stepped forward and placed a hand on her shoulder.

"Jane? Wake up." He tried to use a soft, calming tone, though adrenaline still spurted through him. "Come on, wake up, sweetheart. You're having a nightmare."

Her eyes flickered open and he saw panic and fear in them, then she scrambled to the foot of the bed, kicking and flailing her arms to fight off the perceived attack.

Acting wholly on instinct, he moved in low and grabbed her in a tight hold so she couldn't strike out at him. "It's okay, baby," he murmured. "I'm not going to hurt you."

He crooned nonsense words to her, holding her tight so she didn't hurt him or herself.

Her eyes were huge, dilated with shock and sleep, and he could see instantly when realization hit her. Though she still looked dazed, she shuddered a little then finally went still in his arms.

"Mason?" she whispered

"I'm here. You're safe now."

"They killed him. Dear God, they killed him and I couldn't do anything. All I could do was run as he told me to."

His gut clenched at her words. What the hell kind of trouble was she in? "Who? Your father?"

She blinked at him and whatever shadows were there seemed to be gone as she came back to full awareness. "What?"

"Who was killed?"

She frowned. "Killed? Why would you say that? What makes you think someone was killed?"

He stared at her, frustration growing like an algae bloom. "You just said so. You were talking in your sleep and you said something about how someone killed him and all you could do was watch."

She was starting to look frightened again, only this time, because she was fully conscious, he found it more disconcerting. "I did?"

With great care, he managed to contain his heavy sigh. Every time he thought he might make a little progress discovering clues to her identity, she managed to slap his hopes down.

He released her and slid a safe distance away on the bed. "Have you had any memories of your family?" he asked. "Anything at all that we might use to help figure out who you are?"

She took her time answering. "I had an odd thought yesterday that my father wouldn't have approved of my wardrobe choices. When I tried to put a face to him, I couldn't. I didn't mention it because it seems so foolish and insignificant."

"I don't think it's insignificant at all. You were terrified in your dream. Look at you, you're still trembling."

She lifted her hand into the air and watched her fingers quiver for only a few seconds before she curled them into a fist and folded her arms around herself tightly.

"This is horrible. I'm not sure I want my memory back. What if I don't like what I find?"

To his further self-disgust, her small, frightened admission put him in full protective mode. He couldn't seem to control his actions; it was almost like watching someone else as he pulled her back into his arms.

She settled there just as if she belonged, tucking her head against his chest.

"Hiding from something, even inside your head, won't make it disappear," he murmured.

"Is that what you think I'm doing?"

"Maybe your brain has gone into self-protection mode and is keeping something unpleasant from you because it's too painful to face."

"Something about my father?"

He shrugged. "Maybe. We have no way of knowing for sure until your memory comes back."

"And if it never does?"

Before he could answer, he saw several distant flashes in quick succession, followed by the low rumble of thunder. An instant later, the small lamp by the bed flickered, only this time it stayed off.

Jane stiffened in his arms. "What's happening?"

"The lightning or wind must have knocked the power out. Don't worry about it. The lights will be on again in a moment."

"I hate the dark!"

"It's okay. I've got a flashlight. I left it on the bookshelf."

He moved to retrieve it but she clung to him like a howler monkey.

"Don't leave! Please don't leave me!"

"Okay, okay." He tightened his arms around her, those damn protective instincts buzzing like crazy at the panic clear once more in her voice. "I'm not going anywhere. Easy now. I've got you."

"Thank you. Oh, Mason, thank you."

She seemed to shudder in his arms and then, before he realized what she intended, she pressed her soft mouth to his.

He froze, shocked and dismayed and instantly, painfully aroused. He should stop this, a corner of his brain warned, while the kiss was still tentative and relatively innocent.

But then she drew him closer and murmured his name in that low, sexy British voice and he was lost.

Chapter 10

As her mouth connected with his, Jane felt as if her heart would pound from her chest.

Could he hear it? she wondered, in that tiny instant before he returned the kiss. How could he miss it? The ruckus in her ears sounded like a dozen bass drums beating in unison.

After a moment, she wouldn't have cared if an entire marching band suddenly wandered through. She was too carried away by the avalanche of sensations sweeping her off her feet.

She forgot everything in his arms, forgot the electrical outage, the strain of the last few days, the hundreds of questions she had about who she was and where she had come from.

All she could think of was Mason. In the dark, she was surrounded by him, engulfed by him. She was intensely aware of the solid, comforting strength of his chest against her and she wanted to burrow close to him like a wild creature in need of sanctuary.

He pressed her back against the pillows, his hard, powerful body covering her, and her skin seemed to melt into him. Though the quilt still covered her from the waist down, she could feel heat and energy pouring off him in waves. Her body moved restlessly, eager for more contact.

This was incredible! Was kissing always like this, a wanton rush of heat, this slow churn of blood, the breathless anticipation that something wonderful waited just around some corner?

Somehow she knew their kiss was different. It *had* to be. Wouldn't people want to spend every waking moment with their mouths locked together if it was always like this?

This all seemed so magically new. If she had a husband or a boyfriend tucked away somewhere, wouldn't she remember the intoxicating warmth of a man's body, of strong, hard arms holding her close? Surely these kinds of incredible sensations would be burned into her synapses and not even a head injury could compel her to forget.

She'd ridden that horse today with an instinct and skill she couldn't explain. But here in Mason's arms, she felt an absolute novice. Everything seemed brand-new, a whole wonderful, undiscovered world she couldn't wait to explore.

Breathless and rather dazed, she twisted her arms around his neck and he groaned and deepened the kiss, his mouth hard and urgent. His lips and tongue explored her mouth and she nearly gasped at the wonder of it.

Ah, heaven. She wanted to see him but only a little hazy moonlight shone through the bedroom. Instead of frightening her, the enforced darkness now lent an intimacy to their embrace and she wondered if he ever would have kissed her if the power hadn't failed.

"Say something," he murmured, a rather odd request. His voice sounded raspy, tight, but she found it incredibly erotic—almost as arousing as his hand that suddenly explored her ribcage through the cotton of her borrowed nightgown.

She shivered, her nipples hard and tight and painfully eager. "Touch me," she gasped when his fingers stilled. "Oh, please, Mason."

He made an aroused sound low in his throat and an instant later she gasped again and thought she would faint when his hand cupped the curve of one breast over the soft brushed cotton.

This had to be new. Surely she would have remembered *this!* She felt as if every nerve cell in her body was aflame, as if she would burn away into cinders any moment.

Though her arms still clung tightly around his neck, she bowed back against the mattress to give him more room to maneuver his hand between their bodies, desperately eager for more of those touches.

She completely forgot to breathe when his hand moved to the trio of buttons at the neckline of her nightgown. She waited, stomach muscles tense with anticipation, as he worked them free.

A talented man, that Mason Keller, she thought. How could he manage to work tiny buttons at the same time as his mouth continued its relentless assault on hers?

He had just reached the last one and started to touch bare skin when the lights flickered back on. Later, she wasn't sure if it was the shock of his intimate touch or the unexpected illumination or a combination of both but she jerked, startled, and her head connected smartly with his jaw.

He made a sound of pain and surprise, then rolled away from her, his hand at his jaw.

"Oh! I am so sorry. Are you all right?"

He rubbed his jaw for a moment then worked it back and forth. "I'll live."

"I feel like an idiot."

"You're not an idiot." He paused and in the low light from the lamp, she saw regret filter across those harsh, beautiful features. "I should never have started something inappropriate."

Inappropriate, perhaps, but completely fantastic, she thought.

They fell into an awkward silence. One burning question filled her mind. She had to ask, she thought, or she might very well have to spend the rest of her life trying to find the answer for herself.

"I don't remember kissing," she confessed, her face hot. "Or…or sex or anything. Can you tell me, is it always like that?"

Mason barely heard her question, too appalled with himself and his own actions. She was a guest in his home and he had all but attacked her. In another moment or two he wasn't sure he would have been able to stop.

Finally her question registered and he shifted his gaze to her. She looked flustered, her face adorably pink.

"Like what?" he asked carefully.

"So wonderful." Her voice, that sexy proper British tone, was pitched so low he could barely hear her. "Like Roman candles zinging around in my stomach."

If he hadn't already been aroused and ready to go, her words would have done the trick in an instant.

She looked tousled and beautiful and it took every

ounce of self-control he possessed to keep his hands off of her.

He drew in a ragged breath. He didn't want to see stars in her eyes. She should save them for the kind of man who deserved them. God knows, he certainly didn't.

He wanted to lie, to tell her their kiss hadn't been anything special but the words froze in his throat. He had spent a dozen years doing nothing *but* lie, until even he couldn't remember the truth anymore. So why couldn't he utter the smallest of falsehoods to this woman?

He couldn't do it.

"No. It's not always like that," he finally admitted, his voice gruff.

She digested that for a moment, then she smiled slightly. "I didn't think so. I was certain I should remember if it were."

He absolutely didn't want to think about that, about any unlucky bastard whose kiss she might have forgotten. It was none of his business, he reminded himself. She could have kissed the entire British navy for all he cared.

Like Roman candles zinging around in my stomach.

He pushed her words away. "It shouldn't have happened. I'm sorry. You can be sure it won't happen again."

She compressed her lips together and drew the blanket up to her shoulders. "Of course not."

Mason didn't like this feeling of regret, the odd sense of loss when he walked to the door. He had no business touching her, wanting her. And he sure as hell shouldn't be feeling this tenderness that thrummed through him like a tiny, frantic butterfly.

"It's late. We should both try to get some rest."

"Yes. We should." She tilted her head, studying him

with something in her eyes he couldn't put a name to. "You don't sleep well, do you?"

He blinked at the unexpected question. "What makes you say that?" he asked slowly.

"I heard you moving around downstairs earlier, before I fell asleep. I've heard you every night. You seem…restless."

He didn't know how to respond to that. No way could he tell her she was responsible in part for some of his edginess.

"Does it have anything to do with Charlie and Miriam's parents?"

The question pierced him like a poison-tipped arrow, finding its way instantly to his heart, and his hand tightened on the doorknob. He let out a breath as pain and guilt swamped.

Something about the rain pounding on the window created a cocoon of intimacy in the room and he was stunned at how badly he wanted to tell her about the Betrans.

The fact that he was tempted to confide in her left him unsettled. He shouldn't even consider it. He was a man with many secrets, some he couldn't reveal even on threat of death. The Betrans weren't necessarily in that category but they were part of his life before, a dark world he couldn't talk about.

He had to say something, though. She was watching him expectantly, her blue eyes huge.

"Samuel and Lianne Betran are only two of the many ghosts who haunt me," he finally said.

She must have thought he wouldn't answer. Surprise flickered across her lovely features, followed quickly by a soft, devastating compassion. He tightened his hand on the doorknob, appalled at his fierce urge to sink into that compassion, into her.

He didn't like this tenderness, didn't want it. He certainly couldn't need it—that would make him weak, and he couldn't afford to be weak.

"Good night," he said, his voice brusque. "I hope your dreams are more pleasant the rest of the night."

She drew the quilt around her. "Thank you," she answered after a moment. "And I hope your ghosts leave you in peace."

Little chance of that, he thought, but he nodded and let himself out the door, closing it behind him firmly without looking back.

He checked on the children and found them both sprawled across the *banig* on the floor of Miriam's room. With a sigh—and more of that uncomfortable tenderness—he tugged the pink quilt off Miriam's bed and tossed it over them both then headed for his own room.

There, he stood at the window looking out at the rain again and at the ranch he thought he'd left forever.

He had to hope she regained her memory soon—or played her hand so he knew what the hell her game was once and for all. As he had amply demonstrated tonight, he had no willpower around the woman. He should have left her room the moment she returned to full awareness. He had been caught, though, tangled in a web of intimacy and need and the deep loneliness he didn't want to face.

Somehow Jane made him see all that was missing in his life. Companionship, laughter, the sweet comfort of a woman's touch—all those soft, fragile things he had spent a dozen years convincing himself he didn't need.

He needed to end this somehow, to return things to the way they were before she came to the Bittercreek.

The only question left was how the hell he would accomplish that.

And what he would do when she was gone.

The rainstorm of the night before had blown through, leaving everything on the ranch fresh and clean.

Jane sat on her bed with the window open, breathing in the sweet-smelling air and wishing the storm had done the same to her as it had to the ranch.

She could only hope Mason had slept better than she. Their odd, dreamlike encounter had left her restless and edgy. After he left her room, she had lain in bed for a long time, listening to the rain clicking against the window and trying to ignore the buzz and smolder of her body.

When the hunger seemed to abate and her heartbeat finally seemed to slow to normal, she turned her energy toward straining her brain in hopes of recovering any kind of memory of her past and the events that might have led her to Mason Keller.

She had finally drifted off around the same time the rain slowed, sometime before dawn—only to experience more disjointed, alarming dreams that left her shaken and uneasy.

Now, only a few short hours later, dressed and ready for the day, she sat on the edge of her bed, fighting the temptation to don her nightgown again and sink into the comforting embrace of the bed. Her stomach quivered and her head ached almost as much as it had that first day Mason had found her in the mountains.

It didn't feel like a normal headache, she thought. Pain pulsed from the base of her skull, radiating out in all directions and she was almost certain the headache was causing her nausea.

Even more disquieting than the physical discomfort was her emotional unrest.

She couldn't shake the lingering sensation there was something important she was supposed to remember, something vital her subconscious needed urgently to tell her. She felt as if she were on the edge of recalling…something.

What? She curled her hands with frustration. This was all so maddening. If she had something vital to remember, why the devil couldn't her brain just get on with it? Instead she sat in the guest bedroom of a small Utah ranch, wishing she could just hide here forever, where she was safe.

Safe from *what?*

She shivered, afraid of something she couldn't even name.

This was ridiculous. What did she possibly have to fear? She would probably regain her memory and discover she led a perfectly boring life where nothing exciting ever happened.

She could hope, anyway.

Enough of this maundering. She couldn't stay here all day. Most likely she would feel worlds better once she was up and moving.

She found Pam and the children in the comfortable, inviting ranch kitchen. Pam stood at the big six-burner stove singing lustily along to an American country music song on the radio while Charlie and Miriam watched her, giggling over their heaping plates of pancakes.

Despite her headache, she had to smile at the scene. Just that tiny stretching of muscles sent even more pain radiating through her skull. She couldn't contain a tiny gasp, which drew Miriam's attention first.

The girl smiled at her. "Jane. You are awake. Good morning," she said in English.

"Good morning," Jane replied, forcing a smile.

Pam had stopped her performance at Miriam's greeting and now her gaze sharpened. "Oh, hon. You look awful. Those circles under your eyes are heavy enough to drive a tractor through. You okay?"

"I've a bit of a headache, that's all. And I'm afraid I didn't sleep well. No worries, though. I'll be fine."

"Sit down. You need to get something in your stomach so you can take some aspirin."

Just the thought of food made her stomach roll but the aspirin certainly sounded appealing. She knew Pam was right, taking one on an empty stomach would only make things worse.

Pam set a plate of pancakes down at the table. "Sit down," she repeated. "I'll go see what I can round up in Mason's medicine cabinet."

Jane obeyed—at least the sitting part. Even taking a tiny bite of pancake seemed beyond her capability just now.

The children didn't seem to notice anything amiss. They chattered away in their funny mix of English and Tagalog, though she couldn't seem to focus on what they were saying. She could only be grateful they didn't seem to require any sort of response from her.

Pam returned a few moments later. "I'm afraid you're out of luck. Mason probably hasn't had much time to stock his medical supplies. All I can find are a couple of aspirin in a bottle that was probably past its expiration date the year I graduated from high school."

"I'm sure it will be fine."

Pam made a face. "If you can hang on for five more minutes, I'll run over to our place and find you some Extra-Strength Excedrin. You look like you need it."

Extra-strength *anything* sounded brilliant right about now, especially as the sunlight shining in through the kitchen window stabbed at her eyes with a hundred blades.

She could only nod. "Thank you," she murmured.

Jane managed not to wince when Pam slammed the door on her way out, though it was a near thing. She might have wanted to bang her head against the table a few times but she forced what she hoped was a pleasant expression on her features and turned to the children.

"What are your plans today?"

"Fish," Charlie exclaimed. "Fish, fish, fish."

"I take it you're going fishing," she said dryly.

His vigorous nod left her dizzy. "After Mason meets with the horse doctor."

The veterinarian, she assumed. She hoped everything was all right with his new stallion and that the vet was only there on a routine exam.

"You come fish with us," Charlie said in careful English.

Oh, dear. Wouldn't Mason love to have her tagging along on his grand excursion with his children? Besides that minor detail, she had to assume that at this rate, by the time they left to go fishing, her head would have throbbed completely off her shoulders.

She mustered a smile. "I'd better not," she began, but her attention was suddenly caught by a word or two from the radio announcer.

"FBI agents in the Salt Lake field office say three men are in custody this morning, held on charges related to an alleged plot to steal chemical agents stored at the Deseret Chemical Depot in the west desert. The men, all Vandelusian nationals, reportedly planned to detonate the chemical agents at the scheduled signing next week of an historic trade agreement between the U.S., Great Britain and their country. Our Trudy Gallegos is working on the story and we will bring you more details of this breaking story as they become available."

The bright sunshine of the kitchen suddenly dimmed and the room seemed to spin. The pain in her head crushed out any thought and she had to lay her head down on the table.

"Jane?" Miriam asked suddenly from what sounded like some great distance away. "You are okay?"

She couldn't answer—a thousand images were flashing through her brain so rapidly she couldn't keep up with them, couldn't absorb what they might mean.

All she could focus on was a single word—*Vandelusia.*

The word seemed to ricochet through her brain like a ball in a crazed pinball machine, bouncing off neural pathways, sparking memories here and there.

She knew that word. She knew that country! She'd spent six months in the hot and humid Southeast Asian country the year she turned eleven, while her father was on assignment with the British diplomatic service.

Her father!

Jane lifted her head and clutched a hand to her chest. Her father! She remembered him!

Harry Withington's broad, handsome features formed in her mind, so wonderfully familiar she wanted to weep. Vivid blue eyes, that graying mustache, his wide, open smile.

She only had a brief instant of piercing joy before she remembered the rest. He was dead, she remembered now. That fearless, passionate diplomat had been murdered by rebels in South America while trying to rescue the daughter the rebels held captive.

While trying to rescue *her,* Jane Elizabeth Claire Withington.

She caught her breath as that horrible time hit her with stunning clarity—cowering in that hole where they'd kept her, the six long days she had spent there waiting to die, sure she would at any second.

And then, through a marvelous feat of cunning diplomacy and raw courage, Harry came for her, prepared to negotiate for her release. He hadn't come alone, though, but with a small force of British and American special forces who had been training in the country.

After all this time, Jane could still see the scene vividly in her mind—the sudden glaring shock of sunlight as the material over her hole had been moved aside and then the even greater shock of seeing Harry lean over the edge with his familiar smile.

"Hello, Janie-girl. Shall we go home, then?"

Flat on his stomach in the dirt, he reached down. Still not sure if this was another hallucination, she'd grabbed his hands and a moment later he pulled her out and into his arms.

They had one brief, joyful reunion before all hell had broken loose. She heard a commotion coming from a cluster of buildings and then a moment later three FARC rebels in uniform rushed from the building, weapons at the ready.

"Whoops." Harry's smile looked a little strained around the edges. "I thought we might have a little more time. There's a chopper through the trees there. Run for it!"

She had obeyed on legs weak from hunger, inactivity and unrelenting fear. Just as she'd reached the thick edge of jungle, she heard gunshots.

Only later did she realize Harry had created a distraction to allow her time to reach the helicopter. She saw him go down across the way. She could remember her confusion, her disbelief when he didn't get back up. Why wasn't he coming?

She screamed his name and would have run to him except she'd never had the chance. Suddenly she was surrounded by soldiers. A young American picked her up, screaming and crying, and carried her over his shoulder the rest of the way to the waiting helicopter.

Her last image of her father had been watching out the window of the chopper as the furious rebel leader who had taunted and tormented her for six days fired a gun at point-blank range into his skull.

Dear God. Remembering it now was like watching him die all over again. The same helplessness, the same grief, the same crushing guilt pounded her.

There was more.

She drew in a ragged breath. Terrorists. Vandelusia.

That's why she had been up in those mountains when Mason and the children found her.

Everything rushed back—sitting alone in that restaurant in Park City and overhearing the trade minister, Simon Djami; meeting his gaze and seeing the recognition flash in his eyes as he realized who she was, that she understood every word of their conversation in the obscure Vandish dialect, that she now knew his plans; the cold greasy fear as she was shoved into the cargo area of that lorry.

They had planned to kill her. Only stupid luck—and her father's voice whispering in her ear—had saved her life.

Wave after unrelenting wave of memories washed over her. The lovely cottage on the Thames in Buckinghamshire where she had lived quietly with her mother until Claire Withington died of pneumonia the year Jane turned seven.

The subsequent arrival of the exciting, dynamic father she knew only from rare visits.

How the next eight years of her life were wonderful and horrible at once as Harry dragged her with him to every corner of the world in his work as a troubleshooter in Britain's diplomatic corps.

She had loved being with him but she had been a quiet child who would have much preferred staying in that Bucks cottage to traveling to dangerous locales with exotic food and strange insects.

She remembered everything, from those awful, lonely years after her father died to the present, her tiny flat in London and her stuffy job as a diplomatic interpreter.

She knew exactly who she was now—Jane Withington. Shy, boring and afraid to tumble out of bed most mornings.

She rather thought she liked herself better when she had no memory of that woman.

Chapter 11

"Jane? You must sit. Please, sit."

Though she still felt shaky and disoriented as if she were whirling and spinning through space, she finally keyed into Miriam's frantic words. Jane blinked back to the kitchen of Mason's ranch to find both children gazing at her out of huge, frightened dark eyes.

How long had she been sitting here like an idiot, gazing at nothing but her own sudden wild rush of memories? She couldn't blame the children for their unease.

She mustered a smile, reaching for Miriam's hand and giving it a squeeze. "I'm all right. I'm sorry I frightened you."

Charlie said something in Tagalog that she believed loosely translated to something about having a mouse in his chest. She took that for some kind of idiom she was unfamiliar with about being scared. Oh, dear. Poor thing. She tried to muster a reassuring smile through the tumult of emotions churning through her.

"I'm sorry. I was daydreaming."

She was still trying to reassure them when the door opened and Pam hurried in, a large bottle of painkillers in her hand.

"Sorry it took me so long. Couldn't find them until I remembered I took the bottle along a couple weeks ago when we moved the cattle up to the grazing allotment. We stayed overnight in our fifth wheel, I remembered, so I checked the cabinets in the trailer and voilà. here you go."

"Thank you."

Pam rattled two of them out for her, then quickly poured a glass of water from the faucet. Jane swallowed them quickly, hoping they wouldn't irritate her all-but-empty stomach too terribly.

On the other hand, she couldn't imagine her stomach *not* being upset after what she had just remembered.

"You're looking even more pale. How are you feeling?"

"Not quite ready for the undertaker, I suppose."

Pam smiled. "Glad to hear it, hon. We like having you around, don't we kids?"

The children smiled, though they still looked apprehensive. With a jolt, Jane suddenly realized how her presence here could threaten them

Simon Djami had to be looking for her. She had seen that ruthlessness in his eyes when he'd ordered the others to kill her. Her escape had no doubt infuriated him, and he would still view her as a threat to his plans, a threat that needed to be eliminated.

What if he somehow managed to find her? What if he traced her to the ranch and sent some of his minions for her—or worse, came himself?

She sat at the table, her mind in a panic, until suddenly she remembered the radio broadcast that had started all of this. American authorities had several men in custody, the announcer had said, for plotting the terrorist attack. Somehow they must have uncovered the plot. Did that mean she was safe?

How many men? She tried to remember what the announcer had said. Three, she thought. There had been four men at that restaurant, but she didn't know how many others were involved. Perhaps the others were looking for her.

But why would they bother? She had no other information about the planned attack than what she'd heard on the radio broadcast. She posed no possible threat to them if they were already in police custody.

The realization steadied her and she drew in a deep breath. Where to go from here? Even though the panic receded, she couldn't seem to string two thoughts together with Pam looking on, her features still concerned.

"I think you ought to just go on back to bed," Pam said. "You're not looking at all well."

"No, I'm feeling much better. I swear it. I'll be right as rain in a moment. I can already feel the pills working."

Pam didn't look at all convinced. She opened her mouth to argue but before she could, the door opened and Mason walked into the kitchen.

Her pulse skittered as she remembered lying in his arms the night before and the wild heat between them.

"Okay, the vet's done and I'm ready to go." His smile encompassed even her, Jane was surprised to see, though it seemed slightly wary. "Who wants to go drown some worms?"

She met his gaze, his tentative smile, then felt as if

someone had kicked her hard in the stomach. Blood rushed from her face and the room seemed to spin again as she tried to catch her breath.

She knew him.

That's why he had looked so familiar these last few days, why she had wondered if they had met before. They *had* met. How could she ever have forgotten those eyes, compassionate and hard as flint at once?

He was the young American soldier who had kept her alive by tossing her into that helicopter so many years ago, when she would have run back to Harry, even though it was far too late to help her father.

He had held her while she screamed and cried, while she fought and kicked and pounded on his chest, then while she collapsed from six days of terror, little food and the final shock of watching her adored father die because of her.

She had never forgotten. She had thought of his awkward kindness often over the years and would have tried to thank him for what he'd done for her except she never learned his name, only the nickname "Brick" that the others called him.

She had supposed he had the nickname because he was solid and firm, but now she guessed it had something to do with his given name.

"Jane? Everything okay?"

She was staring, she realized, but she couldn't seem to stop. "I...yes. Fine. Excuse me. I...I need to do something in my room." Like toss her biscuits—or at least the tiny nibble of hotcakes and the two pain relievers burning a hole in her stomach.

She had to get away from here, from the weight of their stares and the questions she wasn't ready to answer.

Her chair nearly tipped over as she scraped it back and she paused only long enough to right it again, then fled the kitchen for the sanctuary of her borrowed bedroom.

Mason frowned at Jane's quick, almost panicked flight from the kitchen. What was that all about? She wouldn't have run out of there any faster if Charlie had suddenly reached over and set her shirt on fire.

"Okay, that was odd," he said to Pam, who was staring after their mysterious houseguest out of eyes wide with worry.

"She said she had a headache. I ran over to our place for some Excedrin and came back with it to find her pale as a ghost and looking like she'd just been slapped upside the head by one."

He thought of that odd, disquieting look in her eyes as she'd stared at him. Something had definitely been different. He couldn't put his finger on what, but the soft woman of the last few days had retreated somewhere inside a skittish, nervous wreck.

What had happened? All he could think about was their kiss the night before. Would that have set her off, turned her into a pale, trembling wraith? He had to doubt it.

Unless he was far more out of practice than he thought, she'd been right there with him, enjoying every second.

Pam and the kids were all looking at him as if he held the keys to the universe and could solve every problem.

"I'll, uh, just go check on her," he muttered.

"I don't think she ate anything to settle those Excedrin. Maybe you ought to take her some toast. Or at least a little of that tea she likes. Let me fix a tray."

She had settled right into his house, hadn't she? He wasn't sure why that pissed him off so much, but he found it extremely annoying that Pam knew exactly what kind of tea she liked.

This had dragged on long enough. He needed answers and he wanted them yesterday.

Five minutes later he stood outside her door carrying an overloaded, frill-bedecked tray like some damn servant in a grand estate somewhere. A footman, wasn't that what they were called? The thought didn't do anything to lighten his mood.

He knocked again, harder this time, and she finally answered, half concealed by the wood-paneled door. She looked pale, almost frightened, he thought. Was she afraid of him? What reason had he possibly given for her to think he might pose any threat to her?

"Pam thought you could use some tea and a little toast."

She made a face, her complexion slightly green. "I'm not very hungry. She didn't need to go to this trouble—I've only a little headache. I told her that but she seems to think food will cure every ill."

"That's Pam for you."

He decided not to wait for an invitation—it was his house, after all—so he just pushed open the door with his shoulder and walked past her into the bedroom.

Inside the bedroom, he wasn't quite sure where to take the conversation, another realization that didn't help his mood. He was a trained spy, an expert at information-gathering. He ought to be able to question her six ways from Sunday, but he discarded every single interrogation technique he thought of using.

He wasn't used to questioning his own methods. But then, he'd never been faced with a subject who affected him like Jane.

Maybe he was turning soft, losing his edge. He sure felt like it standing here in full footman mode, holding a blasted tea tray.

He set the tray on top of the dresser and shoved his hands in his back pockets. "Pam fixed some tea for you. You'd better drink it or you'll hurt her feelings."

She looked like the idea of tea sat her stomach about as well as swallowing a bucket of pig grease but she stepped forward anyway and picked up the cup with elegance and grace, just as he would have expected.

This close to her, he was unnerved to discover how lost she looked—and even more unnerved by his compelling desire to tuck her against him and keep her safe.

He needed her gone from his house so he could get back to figuring out his life!

She took a dainty sip then set the teacup back on the saucer with an absolutely pathetic attempt at a smile. "Thank you. That's delicious. Tell Pam it helped immeasurably."

As if one tiny swallow could take that haunted look out of her eyes. He sighed. "Okay, now that you've fortified yourself with the essential British restorative, you can tell me why you're as jumpy as a grasshopper in a chicken coop."

She focused her gaze on the cup on the tray. "I told you. I've a headache. That's all."

"Sorry, lady. You might be able to sell that to Pam but I'm a little tougher customer. What's going on? Is your memory back?"

Her eyes widened but he couldn't tell whether it was from surprise or guilt before she looked down at her tea again as if it held all the answers to life's mysteries.

"Of course not. Don't you think I would think to mention that tiny little detail to you and Pam and the children if it had?"

He studied her bent head, wondering why she suddenly seemed so fragile. "How would I know what you would or wouldn't do? I don't know a thing about you, Jane—or whatever your name is. You're a bigger mystery to me right now than you were three days ago when I just about ran you down. You want to tell me why that is?"

She lifted her head to meet his gaze and he saw a jumble of emotions in her eyes, most he couldn't identify. "I…I don't know."

"I don't like mysteries. I don't like unknowns. I don't like situations I can't control, and I especially don't like people who lie to me. You're not lying to me, are you Jane?"

"Of course not," she answered with dignity. Still, he wasn't sure he believed her.

He stepped forward and tilted her chin up so she couldn't look away from him again. He needed to see her eyes.

"Tell me the truth. Please. I can't help you unless I know what's going on. Are you in some kind of trouble?"

She said nothing for several seconds, just studied him out of those huge eyes, then she leaned her cheek into his hand for just a brief instant before pulling away.

"I don't know," she whispered. "I can only tell you I truly hope not."

That was no answer at all, he thought.

"Would you tell me if you were?"

"Of course. Why wouldn't I?" She answered just a shade too quickly for him to believe her and he fought the urge to grind his teeth together.

This was getting them nowhere so he abruptly changed tactics. "How's your head?"

She seemed to think about this for a moment, then surprise flickered across her features. "Better, actually. I don't know if it was the Excedrin or the tea but the pain seems to be gone."

"Good," he said, right before he kissed her.

He knew it was a stupid idea even as he did it, but he couldn't resist. He wanted this woman with a fierce need that clutched him by the insides and wouldn't let go.

Is it always like that? she had asked the night before. Her words had haunted him all night and he had known from the moment he walked into the kitchen that he would have to find out.

She stayed frozen in his arms, her body taut with surprise for maybe five seconds, then she wrapped her arms around him and returned his kiss with an ardent enthusiasm that took his breath away.

Back in his Ranger days, whenever his unit had been deployed, he used to watch his fellow soldiers as they were greeted by their wives and their girlfriends on their return. Though he told himself he relished his active bachelor life, in truth he had been deeply envious of those passionate, joyful reunions.

Jane kissed him like one of those soldier's women, as though she hadn't seen him for months and was so grateful to have him in her arms again.

He found it heady, intoxicating, and for several glorious moments they rekindled all the heat of the night before. Some dark and empty place inside him seemed suddenly flooded with light and he wanted to bask in it.

He didn't have much chance before he heard what sounded like two sets of footsteps coming up the stairs. Swallowing an oath, he managed to wrench his mouth away and step back, his breathing uneven and his pulse a loud staccato in his ears.

Jane pressed a hand that trembled slightly to her mouth. Her breathing was ragged, too, he noted, and she had to swallow several times before she found her voice.

"What was *that* all about?"

He raked a hand through his hair. "Damned if I know. You bring out the oddest emotions in me. One minute I want to strangle you, the next I have to kiss you."

"I guess it's good for both of us that I'll be leaving soon, then."

"Right," he muttered, though he had to admit he wasn't particularly thrilled by the reminder. Before he could add anything else, a tentative knock sounded at the door.

In that prim and proper way of hers, Jane took a moment to make sure her shirt was straight and her hair smoothed down before she opened the door. Somehow Mason wasn't a bit surprised to find the children waiting on the other side.

"We will fish now. Let's go," Charlie said.

Mason had to smile at the kid's peremptory announcement. "Eager, are you?"

Charlie nodded. "We fish now. Jane will come, too."

He started to say no, then stopped, considering the idea. He had conflicting goals here. On the one hand, he still wanted to protect the children from future hurt. They had already come to like Jane and having her along on their little trip would only encourage more pain down the road.

On the other hand, he also wanted to figure out what was going on with Jane, why she was so pale and unnerved suddenly. He couldn't do that very well if he was up in the mountains with the kids and she was here at the Bittercreek.

He watched as both children moved toward Jane, drawn to her like tiny creatures to a water source. She laid a gentle hand on Miriam's shoulder and had no problem taking Charlie's undoubtedly sticky fingers in hers. Seeing the three of them together left an odd, unnerving feeling in his gut.

They were already attached to her, he realized, foreseeing trouble on the horizon when she left. What was the point in closing that particular barn door if the horse had already long since run out?

With a feeling he was going to regret this, he turned to her. "You interested?"

She stared at him with shock. "You're asking me to go fishing with you and the children?"

"Is that so hard to believe?"

"Unexpected, that's all." She appeared to consider, then she squeezed Charlie's fingers before releasing them. "I appreciate the offer, but perhaps I'd better stay here."

Charlie shook his head vigorously. "You come. Please."

"Please, Jane," Miriam added.

She studied the two of them and Mason could swear he saw soft tenderness in those blue eyes. "You really want me along?"

"Yes!" the children shouted in unison, throwing their arms around her as if they'd orchestrated it.

With a laugh, she hugged them both to her, then lifted wary eyes to Mason. "Yes. All right. I'll go."

Something was definitely different about her.

He couldn't put his finger on what, but Mason saw subtle changes as he drove his truck up the same mountain road into the Uinta Mountain Range where they had found Jane.

She appeared more thoughtful, more introspective as they drove up the mountains and a few times he thought he saw an awareness—a cognizance—that hadn't been there before.

The children sat between them, Miriam quiet and watchful as usual and Charlie chattering away in his funny, jumbled mix of English and Tagalog. Every once in a while, Mason would take his gaze off the road for an instant to look at Jane and he would find her gazing back at him with an odd, intense look that left him aching and uncomfortable.

Those stars he had seen in her eyes the night before were back a hundredfold, as if the whole universe had unfurled in her gaze in a bright sprawl of glitter.

He didn't know what he might have done to warrant such a look. It wasn't something he was used to—and certainly it was not something he thought he deserved.

She wouldn't look at him that way if she knew him— if she knew who he had been, what he had done.

Of course, he could never tell her. That part of his life was done, sealed forever in the deep, dark morass of intelligence archives. He had a new life now with the children, one he had to hope might eventually allow him to sleep at night.

He could only hope he wouldn't spend the rest of his life dreaming about a blue-eyed Brit.

"Are you sure you know where you're going?" she asked after he turned down another unmarked dirt road.

"It's not far now. I could probably go this route with my eyes closed. My dad took me up here fishing all the time when I was a kid. It was one of the few things we could do together in relative peace."

She looked saddened by that and he thought he saw a spasm of something that looked like grief cross her features. For him? he wondered with some surprise.

He wanted to tell her not to grieve for him, that he and his father had enjoyed a few years of peace before Boyd Keller's heart attack, but the children were looking on curiously and he decided now might not be the most appropriate time to delve deep into his complicated relationship with his father.

"Does any of this look familiar?" he asked instead.

She appeared disoriented by his abrupt change of subject but she looked out the windshield. Did she see the same wild, harsh beauty here that he did? he wondered. The rugged mountains spearing up in the distance, the columbines swaying by the road, the aspens with their pale silver-green leaves and ghostly white trunks.

"No," she said after a long moment. "I don't recognize anything. Should I?"

"You tell me. We're coming on to the place where the kids and I found you Friday."

Had it only been three days? He almost couldn't remember a time when this woman hadn't been part of their lives.

Jane was looking out the windshield again, this time with more interest. He could swear he saw a spark of recognition in her eyes and then a tiny rim of what almost looked like fear.

Frustrated and out of sorts, he pulled the truck to a stop and set the parking brake at exactly the spot where he and the children had nearly run over her as she'd been lying in the dirt.

"Is this it?"

He nodded. "Still no idea what you might have been doing here?"

She said nothing for several moments, then she lifted her gaze to his. "No. None."

As he looked at her, blue eyes so guileless and wide, he couldn't shake the feeling she was lying.

Chapter 12

Even with her now-fully-functioning memory and all the worries that now simmered like a hot, thick soup in her brain, Jane couldn't remember an afternoon she enjoyed more.

On the ride up, as Mason had driven through wild and scenic mountains that seemed like something out of the cinema, she had pored through all her options now that her memory had returned.

She wasn't quite sure what to do. Should she come forward with what she knew? Who would she possibly tell—and what difference would it make, really? According to the radio report that morning, the men were in custody, the plot averted. The world was safe from the Vandelusian Liberation Front for now—or at least the U.S./Britain/Vandelusia trade agreement would be secure, unless Simon Djami had another plan up his sleeve.

The name struck fear in her stomach and she remembered what the radio had said. Three men had been arrested, not the four who had been at that restaurant.

What if Djami wasn't in custody? Would the other men implicate him? She couldn't be sure. She had learned enough traveling the world with Harry Withington to know terrorist cells like the VLF were fiercely loyal, especially to their leaders. The other men would probably rather die than turn against their leader.

If he *was* still free, was it possible he might be looking for her? She was a loose end, someone who could implicate him even if his own men wouldn't. She couldn't imagine someone as ruthless as Djami leaving that loose end untied.

She couldn't let him find her, not when she had two innocent children to protect.

On the other hand, why would he ever think to look for her on a small cattle ranch like the Bittercreek? She couldn't imagine how he could ever possibly find her.

Of course, she couldn't stay at the ranch forever, the lost, pitiful head-injury victim who couldn't remember her own name.

She thought about going forward with what she knew but she had no idea who to tell, who she could trust. Mason had a friend in the FBI, she knew. But along with the return of her memory had come the chilling reminder that Djami had sources in American intelligence circles, too.

That had been one of the most horrifying things about the plot she'd overheard, Djami's complete confidence in the two FBI agents on the VLF payroll, that they would do whatever he asked.

How could she possibly go to the FBI with what she knew when she couldn't be sure which agents could be trusted and which were in bed with Djami and his cohorts?

She desperately wanted to go back to the relative seren-
ity she had enjoyed until that morning, before she had this
cold knowledge in her chest, this heavy responsibility
weighing down on her shoulders.

She would have to do something with what she had
remembered, she knew. Harry Withington's daughter
couldn't let Djami go unpunished, if indeed he was the lone
member of his group not in custody.

However, she couldn't do anything about it at the present. They were in the mountains, miles from anywhere. The
rest of the world seemed far away here and Jane had resolved that she would take one last opportunity to enjoy
the children.

And she *was* enjoying herself. Somehow she managed
to keep the dark clouds at bay and now she and Miriam
were flat on their stomachs on the cool, mossy bank of a
tiny creek, fishing lines stretched out like gossamer spider
webs in the slow-moving water.

A cool, lovely breeze lifted the ends of Miriam's short
hair and the high mountain air was sweet with summer.

Downstream a dozen yards, Mason and Charlie were in
much the same position. She had to admit, she found them
a priceless sight, the handsome, masculine ex-soldier and
an energetic young boy, heads together as they peered into
the water.

Mason's idea of fishing wasn't at all what she might
have expected. Not that she had any experience in pisca-
tory pursuits, of course. Still, on the drive into the mountains she had envisioned some romantic scene of the four
of them standing in a wide, gurgling river, fly rods dipping
and swaying as she'd seen on the telly.

This was stealth fishing, sneaky and sly. Mason had explained that the native trout species in this remote area were easily spooked so they had to be as quiet as possible, an impossible task for Charlie.

The poor boy tried his best but chattering came as naturally to him as breathing, she was afraid.

After an hour at it, she and Miriam had caught two tiny trout between them—both tossed back for being too small as quickly as Mason could help them unhook the slippery devils—while the males were having no luck whatsoever.

"There is one," Miriam whispered, pointing furtively into the crystal water. "You see it?"

Jane followed the direction of her finger and found a plump silvery fish, much bigger than the others they had caught, darting through the swaying water plants.

"Yes," she whispered back. "See if you can move your line a little more toward it."

Miriam nibbled on her bottom lip, propping up on her elbows as she reeled her line so her hook with its juicy worm was closer to the fish. The two of them waited with giddy anticipation for the fish to take the bait.

When it did, Miriam let out a gasp and pulled her fishing pole backward to set the hook. "We caught it!" she exclaimed, reeling the fish out of the water with a low exclamation of delight that drew the attention of Mason and Charlie.

Mason picked up Charlie then made his way across a makeshift bridge made from a downed tree spanning the narrow creek.

"Wow. Look at that! Good job!" he said when he reached them.

"It is very big, yes?"

"This one's a keeper." He grinned at Miriam then pulled

her toward him in a quick, one-armed hug before releasing her so he could unhook the trout and place it in the wicker creel he'd already prepared with a bed of grass. "You can have it for dinner."

Miriam glowed with excitement at the prospect, though Jane had to admit to feeling a little squeamish to think about eating something that had been swimming and frolicking in the water just moments before. A silly way to look at things, she knew, but there it was.

"Why do you catch all the fish?" Charlie asked his sister in Tagalog, his tone piqued. "I want to fish with Jane. She is better at catching the fish."

Mason gave a rueful laugh. "We might have half a chance if you could keep quiet for two seconds at a time, buster."

"You will see, Jane. I can be very quiet," Charlie insisted, zipping his lip and tossing an imaginary key over his shoulder in a gesture Jane guessed he must have picked up from Pam.

She smiled, reaching out to mess his dark hair. "I'm certain you can be still as a mouse, young man. But I didn't have anything to do with catching this fish, I swear. Miriam did it all herself."

The girl beamed and Jane realized with a jolt this was the first time she had seen Miriam wear a full-on, joyful smile like that. The little girl was so solemn, so quietly sad most of the time. It was wonderful to see her glow with happiness.

Emotion welled up in her throat and she did her best to blink back tears. She risked a look at Mason, hoping he had caught a glimpse of Miriam's joy, as well. She needn't have worried. He was gazing at the girl with such a stunned look on his features that Jane abruptly lost the battle with tears.

A few strays slid down her cheeks and she wiped them with a hand that regrettably smelled like trout.

Mason cleared his throat and pulled Miriam into another hug. "Good job," he said gruffly.

He loved these children, she realized. She didn't know the full story as to how they came into his care, but she knew that Mason Keller loved Miriam and Charlie deeply and would do his best to be a good father to them.

She studied him standing by the mountain stream, tall and gorgeous and choked up by a little girl holding a fish, and suddenly made an even more stunning discovery.

She was in love with him.

The truth of her feelings nearly buckled her knees and sent her toppling into the stream. She was in love with him, with a hardened, mistrustful ex-soldier she barely knew.

How could this have happened in only a few days?

No, not a few days. Part of her had always been a little in love with that handsome soldier who had rescued her thirteen years ago and shown her such kindness, who had held her and forced her to drink and tried to comfort her.

He had been the stuff of a girl's dreams, a white knight who had played a part in rescuing her from a horrible ordeal.

Since he'd found her in these mountains three days ago, she had come to know him as much more than just some action-movie sort of hero.

Mason Keller was honorable, loyal. While he hadn't exactly welcomed her into his home, he had treated her with dignity and respect and traces of that kindness he had first demonstrated after her father was killed.

Oh, what a disaster this was turning into. As if she didn't have enough to worry about! Now she had the added complication of knowing her heart was doomed to be broken.

How could the outcome be anything else? Yes, he might have kissed her, but he didn't even know her. Not the real her—Jane Withington, prim and boring and a yellow-livered coward to boot.

He didn't know her, but if he did, she had no doubt he wouldn't like her very much. How could he possibly, when she had come to remember in the last few hours that she wasn't all that crazy about herself?

Harry Withington would have been disappointed in his child. It was a bitter pill. Instead of relishing the life he had sacrificed his own to save, instead of making something worthwhile out of it, she had hidden herself away in her tiny London flat.

She rarely went out, her only friends were superficial ones, and she did her best to fade into the woodwork. She had even done her best to avoid this trip to the States for this historic trade summit but she had been the only translator in the diplomatic pool who spoke Vandish.

If she hadn't come here, none of this would have happened. She wouldn't have been sitting in that restaurant, she wouldn't have been kidnapped by Djami's minions, she wouldn't have met Mason again and these beautiful children.

Her life would have been unbearably dreary—and the sad truth was, if someone had told her a week ago what was in store for her, she probably would have locked herself into her flat rather than get on that airplane.

"You all right, Jane? You're looking a little green around the gills."

She jerked her mind from her grim thoughts and found Mason and the children watching her, wariness in three sets of eyes.

"Yes. Fine, thanks." She manufactured a smile and an

explanation that wasn't wholly a lie. "I've a sudden feeling I'm not particularly fond of trout after all."

"That's okay. We'll eat your share, won't we kids?"

Charlie and Miriam both giggled.

"So what do you say we switch fishing buddies for a while?" Mason asked. "I'll take Madame Trout-slayer here and you can try your luck with the chatterbox."

"Fine," she murmured, already grieving at the thought of leaving the three of them, of returning to that pitiful excuse for a life.

He had missed these mountains, Mason acknowledged a few hours later. Missed the purity and the peace, the quiet and the vastness.

Sitting here by a mountain stream with his hands around a fishing rod and his lungs filled with sweet mountain air, he could almost forget about the scars and burns on his soul. They were there, always there, but for the first time he started to wonder if maybe some of the worst of those wounds might start to heal.

With a sigh, he cast out again, not far but enough that his line landed just upstream of an oxbow in the stream where the water ran deep and slow. If he wasn't mistaken, that looked like the perfect place for a nice big trout to lurk and enjoy a summer afternoon.

He had to admit, he'd had better luck the last hour without the kids.

The children had proved to have short attention spans when it came to the ancient art of angling. They had fished for a while but had grown bored with it.

After their lunch of cold cut sandwiches and potato salad packed by the redoubtable Pam, Charlie had moved upstream where the stream was wider and more shallow. He had waded into the icy mountain water and tried his luck catching fish with his bare hands—without much success but to everyone's great amusement.

Miriam had spent a long time gathering an armload of brilliantly colored wildflowers, then fashioned a makeshift vase for them from her juice bottle. That task done, she curled up on a blanket Mason had spread out in the shade while Jane read aloud to her from a Harry Potter book Pam must have tucked in the picnic basket.

He was too far away to hear the story but he didn't need to. Just imagining her sexy voice reading the words was enough to send heat sizzling through him and he wished he dared stretch out in the shade along with them.

After a while, Charlie joined them on the blanket, his head cuddled on Jane's lap. The sight did funny things to Mason's insides and he had to look away.

He needed to do more of that with the children, Mason had thought. It would help their English if he set aside a regular reading time each day. The only trick was trying to fit it into their hectic schedule, but he would have to make time, he decided.

The next time he risked a look at the children, he saw that the afternoon warmth and the day's excitement had been too much for them. They were both sound asleep.

A moment later, Jane rose quietly and came over to join him by the water's edge. He handed her the other fishing rod, but she seemed content just to sit and watch him, her arms wrapped around her knees and her features pensive.

Just now, she looked like she ought to be back on the blanket curled up with Charlie and Miriam.

"You can stretch out if you'd like," he murmured. "There's another blanket in the truck."

She blinked a few times and he was fascinated by the hint of color crawling across those lovely, elegant cheekbones. "I'm sorry," she murmured with a hastily covered yawn. "It's been an…eventful day."

"Go ahead. I don't mind. I'm about fished out myself. I figured we'd start heading home when the kids wake up."

"I don't want to sleep." Her smile was sheepish. "I'm enjoying this too much."

Her admission surprised and pleased him. He would have felt the loss if she decided to nap with the children, he acknowledged. Just having her near him had an odd, calming effect on him. He wasn't sure he cared for it.

He hadn't made much progress figuring out why she seemed so different today. He was just about to push the matter when she smiled suddenly, unexpectedly, and he had to ask why.

"I was just remembering something Charlie told me while we were fishing together. A joke he learned from Pam."

"The one about the fish and the ice-cream cone?"

She giggled. It was the only word he could use to describe her delighted gurgle. "I guess you've heard it, then."

"Yeah. I have a feeling I'll be hearing more than my share of bad jokes the next few years."

Her eyes softened as she studied him. "You're crazy about them, aren't you?"

He thought of how his world had changed in the past four months, how the things that had always seemed of life-or-death importance to him had faded in significance.

It was a completely novel experience. Was this what all parents went through? He wondered. This subjugating of their own wants to make sure their children had what they needed?

"Yeah," he said gruffly. "Pretty crazy."

"They love you, too. Whatever you might think, you're doing a good job of parenting them. I know it can't be easy for you."

"I'm learning. I'll never be the parents Samuel and Lianne were, but despite my shortcomings, I have to believe they're better off here than in some orphanage."

"Samuel and Lianne. Those were their parents?"

She had asked him before about the Betrans and he had avoided the subject. Here in the solitude and peace of the mountains, he thought perhaps the time had come to talk about them. He couldn't help wondering if, by opening up to her about this part of his life, he might inspire her to do the same.

"Yeah. They were great people. Samuel was a lawyer in the Mindanao region. A good one. And Lianne taught school."

"How did you meet them?"

Ah, here the ground turned a little soggier. "He represented me when I had a little legal trouble."

"Nothing serious, I hope?"

"No. Just some minor infractions." That had been his cover, anyway. In his role as a disreputable tavern owner, he had run afoul of the local cabal that passed for law enforcement in the area. He and Samuel had used legal consults as their excuse to pass information.

"You cared about them, too," she said softly. "That's why you've taken their children."

In the intelligence-gathering business agents weren't supposed to care about anything but doing the job. He had broken those rules with the Betrans. Somehow their decency, their kindness had drilled through all of his barricades.

"What happened to them?"

He didn't answer for a long time, listening to the soft music of the stream and the wind's lonely mourn in the treetops. Finally he reeled his line in and set it aside, his gaze on the mountains surrounding them.

"They were targets of a terrorist attack," he said, his voice low. "A car bombing."

She made a soft sound of distress and looked quickly toward the sleeping children, sorrow and something else that looked like guilty unease in her eyes.

"I'm so sorry. The children weren't in the car, I hope?"

He picked a blade of snakegrass and rolled it between his fingers. "They were in a safe house. Samuel had begun to suspect their lives might in danger so he took measures to protect the children. He and Lianne were heading to a different safe house but the terrorists found them first. Just as he feared they would."

Even to his own ears, his voice sounded harsh, bitter. He couldn't help it. He *felt* harsh and bitter whenever he thought about the Betrans and their sacrifice that had been as needless as it was tragic.

He should have *done* something. Instead he'd stood by while two decent people—two people far better than he— had been killed for what they believed.

So much for his theory that being here in the mountains might help those scars on his soul heal a little. This one would never go away.

To his shock, Jane reached over and laid a hand on his forearm. "You blame yourself, don't you?"

He looked down at her slim, pale hand against his skin,

a lump in his throat and familiar guilt in his stomach. "With good reason."

She was waiting for him to tell her the rest of it, he knew. How much could he reveal when most of his activities in the country had been clandestine—and very classified?

"In addition to the legal end of things," he finally said, "we worked together on some projects for the government. Samuel had begun to fear he might become a target of terrorists because of... some information he had. He came to me for help getting his family out of the country. I tried. But not hard enough. They were killed before I could put the wheels in motion."

"So you brought their children to the States."

It hadn't been anywhere near as easy as that simple sentence might suggest.

He had spent weeks filling out paperwork, trying to convince the Philippines government that it would be in the best interest of the children to allow a single American man to adopt them and take them out of the country. It had taken a complex combination of bribes and coercion and even then the odds of him succeeding would have been slim to none if he hadn't had a will drawn up by Samuel just before his death naming Mason guardian of Miriam and Charlie.

To this day, he wasn't sure whether his friend's last legal act had been a gesture of desperation or a twisted sort of revenge.

"Did you quit your military service, then, to bring them here?"

He was so busy listening to the way she said "mili-tree" that it took a while for her actual words to register.

"How did you know I was in the military?" He scoured

his memory to see if he'd mentioned anything about it to her. He didn't think he had. His time as a Ranger wasn't something he tended to bring up in conversation.

She didn't look at him, her gaze was fixed on the rippling water. "Pam told me, I think. Yes, I'm sure of it. She mentioned you were in some kind of special forces. Army Rangers, I believe."

He thought of his extensive cover the last few years, of a feckless American barkeep interested only in booze and women. The layers of untruths that had surrounded him. How different would his life have turned out if he'd stayed in the army? He doubted he would have to live with a tight knot of shame for some of the things he'd done.

"Rangers. Right."

"Do you miss it?" she asked.

He had no answer to that. His time as a Ranger seemed another lifetime ago. As to the other, did he miss it? Sometimes, he had to admit. Despite the dark edges, there had been a furtive kind of thrill to it, to outsmarting genuine enemies and coming out on top, believing what you were doing would make the world a little more safe.

For all that, he was glad to be out of it. And who knows? Someday he might even feel clean again.

He pushed the thought away, wondering how this conversation had turned a one-eighty on him. He was supposed to be subtly putting his interrogation skills to work on Jane. So why was he the only one spilling any information here?

"That part of my life is over now. I'm doing my best to make a different sort of life here for me and the kids."

She rested her chin on her shoulder and gazed at him, her eyes looking impossibly blue in the sunshine and her dark hair lifting a little in the breeze. He abruptly realized what the poets meant by drowning in a smile. He could feel himself going under, sliding toward oblivion.

How could he feel such tenderness toward a woman he didn't know? He wanted badly to trust her, to believe she was the innocent creature she appeared. The strength of that desire left him weak and stunned.

"You're a remarkable man, Mason Keller."

"No. Just a man," he murmured, right before he kissed her.

Chapter 13

Jane held her breath as his arms wrapped around her, as his mouth found hers with a slow gentleness that for some ridiculous reason brought tears to her eyes.

He made no move to deepen the kiss, only held her close, his body warm and solid and comforting while the stream rippled beside them and the wind soughed and sighed.

Emotions poured through her, welled up inside her. Oh, how she loved this man. The force of it left her weak and trembling and hurting already with the inevitability of their parting.

"Whoever you are, Jane Doe, I'm beginning to think you've got some magic in your blood," he murmured against her mouth.

Dazed, almost numb, she could think only of her prosaic, boring life in England. Magic? She hardly thought so. "Why would you say that?"

He smiled a little, his silvery eyes reflecting the sunshine, and pulled her into his lap. "I certainly don't have amnesia. But every time I kiss you, I can barely remember my own name."

She had no response to that so she did the only thing that came to mind. She kissed him. Filled with a heady sense of power from his words, she twisted her arms around his neck and poured all the emotions she couldn't express with words into her kiss.

Underneath it all was a deep, wrenching sorrow. As wonderful as this was to find herself in his arms, the moment was as fleeting as a leaf bobbing upon the stream.

In an instant, it would be gone and she would be left with only the memory of how much she loved him—a memory she knew nothing could take from her, not all the head injuries in the world.

She kissed him fiercely and his response was immediate and gratifying. He made a low sound of arousal deep in his throat and pulled her closer.

"Jane—" he started to say but before he could complete the thought, they both heard a rustling in the tall meadow grass. The children! She'd completely forgotten about them.

Jane scrambled off his lap just as Charlie reached them. He appeared to find nothing odd in the last seconds of the kiss he must have observed.

"I catch more fish now," he announced, then picked up his fishing pole and headed toward the water's edge.

Jane had to swallow a laugh at his matter-of-fact tone. Mason let out a heavy breath then lifted the coffee can full of worms, a wry expression replacing the one of desire he had worn just seconds before.

"You gonna want a little bait on that hook, pal, or are you trying a dry run?"

Charlie appeared to weigh his options. "You put worm on," he finally declared.

Jane had to hide her smile at his peremptory tone, which reminded her a great deal of the elderly matrons who had flats in her building and delighted in ordering the doorman about.

Mason rubbed the boy's sleep-mussed hair. "You can fish for a little while, then we're going to head back to the ranch, okay?"

Charlie nodded. Jane thought he would turn to the fishing with his usual rapid-fire enthusiasm for everything, but he paused then rested his head against Mason's arm for a long moment in a gesture of trust and affection that brought those dratted tears back to her eyes.

Mason was touched as well, she saw. He swallowed hard and remained still until Charlie reached for the baited pole and headed off.

Oh, she was in trouble. Bad enough that she most likely had international terrorists after her. She was deeply in love not only with an ex-soldier who still exuded danger, but with his two wounded children, as well.

She would have to leave all of them, she knew, and her heart broke all over again.

Their fishing trip into the mountains resulted in some elemental shift in matters between them.

On the drive back, Mason tried to put a finger on what, exactly, had changed. He felt as if he had traveled over some invisible bridge. Behind them lay all the suspicion and mistrust and ahead of them stretched out…what?

He wasn't sure and wasn't even certain he wanted to

think about it. He couldn't seriously be considering anything with this woman. She didn't even know her own name! How could he even look at a future with her when her past was a big blank wall?

Still, over the last few hours, he had come to the realization that he trusted her. He never would have told her about Samuel and Lianne if he hadn't.

How had it happened? Had it been while he had watched her kindness and patience with the children as they fished together? Or while she picked wildflowers with Miriam or snickered at Charlie's joke?

She had treated the children with kindness, patience and affection. How could he help but trust her?

He had to believe everything had happened as she had told them. She had no memory beyond that moment he had found her on the road. She didn't know why she had been here or who she might have been before.

He had to work harder to figure out her identity. He still had connections. Surely he could find *something*. Daniel hadn't run her fingerprints. They could start there and see if anything turned up, though he didn't have the highest of hopes.

He also hadn't followed up with Cale about those diplomatic papers she had mentioned. It was a slip-up that bothered him, a detail he never should have overlooked.

He had to wonder if some part of his subconscious didn't *want* to know who she was, wary of what he might find if he poked under too many rocks.

The time for games, subconscious or otherwise, was over. They had to figure out who she was and end this. He resolved to make two calls as soon as they returned to the ranch—he would talk to Daniel about coming out to the ranch with a fingerprint kit, and he would tell Cale about a possible diplomatic tie.

Neither prospect appealed to him much but he knew he had no choice in the matter.

He found he wasn't eager to return to the ranch, for their time together to end. As they drove under the carved log proclaiming the Bittercreek, his hands tightened on the steering wheel and a vague sense of foreboding settled in his gut.

"Thank you for a lovely day," she murmured as they approached the ranch house. "I can't say when I've had a more enjoyable one."

His laugh was short. "Considering you can only remember back a week or so, I'm not sure that's saying all that much, is it?"

She let out a long breath and when she turned to him, he thought he saw shadows in her blue eyes. "Something tells me this is the best day I've had in a long, long time, Mason."

He *had* to find out who she was, for her sake as much as his own.

"Good." His voice came out gruff enough that Charlie laughed.

"You sound like the bullfrog." The boy's little face lit up with a grin and Mason had no choice but to smile back.

"Ribbit. Ribbit," he said in the same gravelly voice, sending both children into peals of laughter. Charlie stopped long enough to make a high-pitched ribbit of his own and even Miriam joined in, though her frog was small and ladylike.

After a moment, Jane gamely tried one, too, and when Mason braked in front of the ranch house, it sounded like an entire amphibian colony had taken up residence in his truck.

"Looks like Pam's gone home for the day," he observed. "Her car's gone, anyway."

Jane laughed. "I suppose that's a good thing. With all this ribbiting, she'll think we've all gone barmy in the mountains."

He had a feeling he, at least, had done just that.

"Okay, kids. We need to carry in all this stuff and then you both can help me cook up our catch."

With all of them working together, it wouldn't take long to unload the truck. He handed Miriam and Charlie the blankets and jackets to carry in between them, and loaded Jane up with the fishing equipment.

He was dumping the ice from the cooler into the flowerbeds when his cell phone bleated at him. The sound startled him and he realized how long it had been since he'd heard that distinctive ring.

He pulled it from his pocket. "Yeah."

"Keller. It's Cale Davis. Where the hell have you been all afternoon?"

That premonition he'd had on the way home returned full force as he picked up the urgency in his friend's voice.

"I've been up in the Uintas. I guess I must not have cell service up there. What's going on?"

"Oh, not much. Only that I think I know the identity of your mystery guest."

He inhaled swiftly, then could have kicked himself for not concealing his emotion. He didn't need the sharp-eared Cale Davis jumping to any inappropriate conclusions.

He leaned a hip against the tailgate and tried to make his tone noncommittal, indifferent, even. "Oh?"

"Are you sitting down?"

Jane came out just then for another load and he handed

her the picnic basket and waited until she returned to the house before speaking again.

"Close enough," he growled. "Just give it to me."

He had the oddest feeling, it was as if he were standing on the edge of a precipice, staring down at an endless drop.

"First I've got to ask if you've been listening to the news today?"

"No. Why?"

"Your old stomping grounds is in the local news today. Didn't you spend a year or two in Vandelusia?"

He thought of warm white beaches and exotic, unspoiled beauty. When he had lived there, most people had welcomed the Americans. Over the last few years, Vandelusia, like other Southeast Asia countries, had become a hotbed of terrorist activity. Though the government was working hard to crack down on it, they had a long road ahead.

"Yeah," he answered, trying to figure out where all this was going. "They're supposed to sign a trade agreement with the U.S. and Britain in a couple days, right?"

"When they do, they can thank the U.S. government and its nifty little web of informants that the event is a celebration instead of a holy nightmare. Ever heard of the VLF? The Vandelusia Liberation Front?"

"Sure. A particularly nasty faction with an increasing presence in other South Asia countries."

He tried to remember the most recent FactSheet before he left the business. The VLF wanted the small, emerging country to shun all western influences and become an isolated regime. Their leader was a mysterious, shadowy figure believed to hold a position of power in the government.

"It hasn't been pinned down but it's believed they have ties to both Jemaah Islamiyah and al-Qaeda."

"We have three Vandish men linked to the VLF in custody today after they managed to break into the Deseret Chemical Depot and sneak out with a canister of nerve gas. They planned to detonate it right in the middle of the treaty signing."

Mason growled a furious oath. How many lives would have been lost if they had succeeded? He hated thinking about it, especially since the trade summit was to be held just over the mountains from here in the resort town of Park City.

So much for thinking he would bring the children home where they would be safe from that world. Nowhere was safe, he thought grimly. Not when the terrorists had schematics of American schools on their computers and when crop dusters that could be used to deliver biological or chemical weapons turned up missing from the heartland.

He fought down a grim sense of hopelessness at ever defeating such hatred and tried to put the pieces together.

"What does all this have to do with my Jane Doe?"

"Jane is her name, all right. Convenient alibi, isn't it? Not so much to remember that way. But I wouldn't be so quick to claim her as yours."

His hand tightened on the phone and his guts twisted with a sense of impending disaster. "What do you mean?"

"Jane Withington, a British translator connected to the trade summit, has disappeared. She didn't show up for work two days in a row before someone thought to report her missing and it was another day before the local yokels thought to bring in the Feds. During the investigation into her disappearance, we found evidence in her Park City hotel room that connects her incontrovertibly to the VLF. She was the one set to detonate the nerve gas device."

The world seemed to gray around him and he couldn't breathe, couldn't think. It was impossible. It *had* to be impossible.

Fast on the heels of that was an all-consuming fury. It roared through him like a brush fire on a hillside of dry sage. She had lied to him. She had looked at him with innocent eyes, had slept in his house, had played with his children.

Jane Withington.

He rolled the name around in his head. He knew that name somehow but he couldn't seem to think past the rage. Maybe she was on a watch list he'd seen.

He had to clear his dry throat twice to get any words out. "What would she be doing here?"

"Good question. I'm not directly involved on the task force and I'm getting everything secondhand but it's believed she had a falling-out with other members of the cell and perhaps went into hiding."

"How do you know it's the same woman?"

"I've seen her papers, Mason. Jane Withington is twenty-eight years old with brown hair and blue eyes, five three, a hundred ten pounds. Sound like your mystery guest?"

"And thousands of others."

"How many of them have British accents and happen to speak Vandish and according to her papers at least a dozen other dialects, including Tagalog, Parsi and Arabic?"

Nausea churned through him. He didn't want to believe this. *Couldn't* believe it.

"Look," Cale said at his continued silence, "do you have a secured fax? I can send you her photo and then you'll know for sure."

He hated himself for holding on to any tiny shred of hope that this was all some horrible mistake but he had to be sure.

"Yes. Send it." He gave Cale the number.

"Okay, give me a second," the FBI agent said.

By the time Mason walked numbly into his office, he could hear the fax machine whirring. After the longest thirty seconds of his life, the machine spat out a page. His heart pounding, Mason picked it up and watched that shred of hope crumble into nothing

Jane gazed back at him, though the grainy fax did nothing to capture her soft beauty or the way her eyes could light up one moment and go dark with sadness the next.

Damn her. It was all an act. Everything, from the moment he found her on the road to their slow kisses that afternoon.

He scrubbed a hand over his face hard enough to leave marks in his skin. This was a frigging nightmare.

"Mason? Are you there?" Cale asked in his ear and Mason realized he had never disconnected the cell connection.

"Yeah." His voice didn't sound like his own.

"Did you get the fax?"

"I did."

"Can you verify the woman staying in your house matches that photograph?"

It sure didn't show what a hell of an actress she was, how her eyes could soften with vulnerability and her mouth could seem as innocent as a day-old kitten's.

She had listened to him talk about terrorists today, about the Betrans, and had seemed so damned sympathetic. All the while she was part of the VLF, which was strongly linked to Jemaah Islamiyah and no doubt Abu Sayyef, the shadowy group responsible for that car bombing.

"Mason? You still there?" Cale asked again.

He shoved his fury away and yanked himself back to the conversation. "Yeah. I'm here. It's her."

Though he tried to be cold and emotionless, something in his voice must have alerted Cale to the wild rage prowling around inside him. When his friend spoke, his voice was low. "I'm sorry, man."

"So am I," he said briskly. "Want me to bring her in?"

"That's going to be tricky. I haven't told anybody you've got a British woman staying at your ranch. We need to figure out how to play this to keep you out of it."

He appreciated Cale trying to protect him but he saw the implications clearly. He was a former intelligence operative who had left the business under less than ideal circumstances—a handy little euphemism that covered the fact that he had pissed off just about everybody he'd ever worked with by quitting the game in midplay.

"I've been harboring a suspected terrorist for three days. No matter how you spin it, I'm going to be dragged in, whether I like it or not."

"We can at least try to minimize your involvement."

"Just what is my involvement?"

"I can testify that you didn't know her identity, that you came to me for help the first day you found her," Cale said. "That should help a little."

Mason sighed. The first shock of rage had passed and he felt battered by it. He felt at least a hundred years old, worn and tired.

"Just come and get her."

He thought for a moment. He wasn't ready to just hand her over to the authorities. That would be too entirely simple, too clean for her. No, she had dragged him into this and he deserved to know why.

"How long will it take you?"

"Half an hour, maybe. As soon as I notify the task force, I'm sure they'll put a rush on sending agents to get her."

"I need a favor. See if you can stretch it out to an hour, will you?"

Silence met his request. "Are you sure that's a good idea?" Cale finally asked.

"What? I only want a few minutes to talk to her."

"Only talk?"

"You think I'm going to break out the rubber hose? Yes, just talk. The woman made a fool out of me and put the kids in danger. I just want to know why."

"I'll see what I can do about stalling for a half hour but I can't make any promises."

"Thanks."

Mason ended the call and set his phone down carefully on his desk next to that grainy fax.

The woman gazing up at him from that image was a stranger. He thought he had come to know Jane in the last three days. He had laughed with her, had shared her nightmares, had even shared some of his own.

An illusion. All of it. How the hell had he allowed himself be so taken in by her?

What was she after here? He didn't think it could be revenge. He had never investigated VLF—or not directly, anyway. Abu Sayyaf had been his chief area of expertise.

He could think of no information he possessed that they might find of interest.

And what about her head injury? As Lauren said, X-rays didn't lie but one solid thunk with a metal pipe wielded by friend or enemy could have done the same kind of damage. Maybe it was part of some elaborate plan to infiltrate his household, though he couldn't begin to guess why she might want to.

His fury seemed to hit him in waves. The initial assault was done, but now he could feel more anger building. Cale's delay would only buy him a few minutes. He didn't have much time to figure out what game she played—and why she had chosen him as one of the other players.

He found her in the kitchen with the children. All three of them had aprons on and Jane stood at the sink running water over a strainer full of vegetables.

He stood and watched them together for a full sixty seconds, while she laughed at something the children said, while they smiled at her and at each other, thoroughly content with her company.

Deceitful, lying bitch.

She had fooled them all, he thought as bitter fury gnawed holes in his heart.

Charlie caught sight of him first. "We make the salad to go with the fish. You cook it now?"

"In a minute." It took every ounce of control for him to keep his voice calm. "Miriam, can you look after your brother for a few minutes and carry on here with the salad? I need to talk to Jane."

"Yes, sir," Miriam said, her wise old eyes suddenly apprehensive at something in his tone or his body language.

Jane followed him from the room. His lungs felt tight, oxygen-starved, so he'led the way out onto the wide porch overlooking the mountains.

"You look upset," Jane said as soon as the door closed behind them. "Everything all right, then?"

"Just great. Brilliant, isn't that what you Brits say?"

With the savage fury still churning through him, Mason

decided it would be better all around if he maintained a safe distance between them, though it took all his control not to shake her until her teeth rattled out. He moved ten feet away and leaned against the porch railing.

She watched him go, blue eyes dark with sudden wariness. "What's happened? Why are you angry?"

"You tell me, *Jane*."

He knew.

Something about that peculiar emphasis he placed on her name sent all the blood rushing from her head and she felt herself sway.

Perhaps it wasn't what he said or how he said it so much as that hard, implacable light in his eyes.

He had taken a phone call. Whoever had rung him up had given him information about her. Why that should make him so angry at her, she couldn't guess. Maybe he feared, as she did, that her presence here might bring danger to his family.

She couldn't think what to say, where to begin so she just gazed at him in helpless misery.

"Why here? Why me?"

His voice stropped her nerves like a sharpened blade and for a long moment she could only stare at him blankly. "S-sorry?"

"Why did you have to drag me and my family into this? Those children in there have been through enough, damn you."

He was right, she had put the children in unnecessary danger. She had no defense to offer so she tried to think what Harry Withington would do. He was a genius at diplomacy, at smoothing out rough waters. She could certainly use his help now.

She did her best to try for a noncommital tone. "I'm not sure what you're talking about."

"Bullshit."

The curse word hit her like a shotgun blast and she flinched.

"You're Jane Withington, aren't you?" he asked.

Twelve hours ago she had been plain Jane Doe. Mysterious, maybe, certainly untrustworthy. But at least he hadn't looked at her with this consuming hatred.

She let out a breath and sagged onto a rocker on the porch. "How did you know?"

"You picked the wrong man to screw with, lady. Next time maybe you ought to pick somebody without connections."

She wasn't quite sure what that meant. But then, she wasn't sure what *any* of this meant.

"So you know everything, then? About the…the planned attack at the trade summit?"

He blinked at her words as if he hadn't expected them. Perhaps she'd been wrong. Perhaps he didn't know everything.

"I know everything I need to. Your name is Jane Withington and you're connected to a VLF cell with plans to carry out a chemical attack aimed at preventing the signing of a trade agreement between Vandelusia and several western countries."

Her laugh was short, harsh. "Connected to them? I suppose that's one way to put it."

"How would you put it?"

"They tried to kill me! If not for a broken lorry door and a rattly mountain road they would have succeeded!"

Chapter 14

He folded his arms across his chest and leaned against the porch railing, his expression as hard and unmoving as the mountains around them.

"Let me guess. You're just an innocent bystander, dragged into their hatred and conspiracies against your will."

"Yes! Exactly!"

"Nice try. Just answer my question. Who leaked my identity to you and put my family in danger? And why the hell did they want to drag me into this?"

She tried—and failed—to puzzle through his words. What difference would his identity make? It was sheer coincidence that he happened to be the one who found her.

"I don't know what you're talking about," she admitted. "All I know is that three days ago, I knew exactly who I was. Jane Withington, an interpreter with the British diplomatic corps. My life was safe and rather boring, just as I liked it, until I happened to be sitting in a Park City restaurant and overheard four men talking in Vandish—which unfortunately for me, happens to be one of the languages with which I am familiar."

"And?"

"And they kidnapped me and stuffed me in the back of the lorry so they could kill me and drop my body where it wouldn't be found. Only I somehow managed to get free before they could carry out their plan."

"Assuming I believe your story—which I don't—that explanation still begs the question of why, in the last three days, you didn't come forward to the authorities with what you heard."

"I had amnesia! You know I did! I didn't remember any of this until this morning when I heard a radio report that three Vandish men had been arrested."

"Is that right?" His tone and skeptical expression clearly demonstrated he didn't believe a word she was saying.

"I didn't! I swear it. All I remember is trying frantically to escape, knowing they would kill me as soon as the lorry stopped. I didn't want to die. Not like that, like—" *my father,* she started to say but the words tangled on her tongue.

"While I was trying to figure out how to escape," she went on after a pause, "I discovered the doors weren't latched properly and somehow I was able to push them open from the inside. I'm still not sure how. Things are hazy from there, but I think I remember falling out. I must have hit my head because the next thing I remember is waking up to find you standing over me. Then I heard that radio report and everything came flooding back."

"Convenient for you, your memory coming back all in a rush like that, right before the net closed around you."

She shivered at his cold words. "Convenient? I was terrified when I remembered! It was like going through it all over again. None of this seems real. It's like some horrible nightmare."

A nightmare she had lived before, but she wasn't prepared to share that with him now. Not when he was looking at her with such cold fury.

"It's real enough. And thanks to you, I'm in it now. Who gave you my name?" he asked again, and she grieved for the disappearance of the man who had held her and kissed her so tenderly not two hours before. There was no trace of him in this hard, dangerous man.

"No one! Why would anyone? Mason, you must believe me. If I had remembered for one second there might be VLF terrorists after me, I would never have come here. I would never deliberately put you and two innocent children in harm's way."

"Sorry, sweetheart, but I'm done believing you. You might as well save your lies for the FBI."

"FBI?"

"You didn't think I was going to let you just hang around on the ranch for another week or two and play with my kids until you decided you were bored, did you?"

It is good you have bought the loyalty of your two FBI lapdogs.

She could hear that VLF terrorist's words as clearly as if he were standing beside her. Fear grabbed her in a stranglehold. If Djami had FBI agents on his payroll, she would be no more safe in FBI custody than she'd been in the back of that lorry.

"No! You can't do that. Please, Mason!"

At her words, a light she hadn't noticed before seemed

to blink out. She realized how her words must have sounded to him, that she was guilty and afraid to face justice.

That tiny spark had been hope, she realized, despair thrumming through her. He hadn't wanted to believe she was guilty but everything she said seemed to point in that direction.

His words confirmed it. "Now why would an innocent woman be so afraid of dealing with the FBI? It's not like they're going to shove bamboo shoots under your fingernails to make you talk or anything. Oh, I forgot. You have nothing to tell them, do you?"

Should she tell him all she had learned that night? She didn't want to drag him in further, to possibly endanger him with her knowledge but right now he was the only person she could trust. She had no choice.

"I've had a great deal of time to think about this since I heard the radio report this morning. I realized that only three of the four men I know to be involved are in custody. I suspect I know which one is not."

She thought of Simon Djami, of the chilling indifference in his eyes when he ordered his henchmen to take her into the mountains and kill her. He had seen her as nothing more than an annoying bug to be squashed.

"I know who the mastermind is behind the attack and who's secretly leading the VLF. Why do you think they tried to kill me?"

"I only have your word that they did."

"I swear it's the truth. And if you turn me over to the FBI, they'll succeed. I won't live long enough to share what I know with anyone."

"What are you talking about?"

"When I was in that restaurant overhearing them, the

leader claimed two FBI agents were helping him. His 'paid lapdogs,' they called them.''

He shook his head, mouth curled with disgust. "You are a piece of work, lady. Don't you know when the game is up? You really expect me to believe two U.S. intelligence agents were profiting from a plot to launch a chemical attack inside our borders? Sorry, sweetheart. I'm not buying."

"All I know is what I heard. If you turn me over to the FBI, I know Djami will find a way to kill me."

"Djami?"

"Simon Djami. The Vandelusian trade minister. He's the fourth man I saw in that restaurant."

He wasn't buying any of this. She could see the disbelief and anger in his eyes and wanted to weep at it. Though she had virtually been on her own since she was fifteen, she had never felt so horribly alone.

"You have to believe me, Mason," she pleaded. "You're the only person I can afford to trust. You were an Army Ranger. You could help me escape!"

He stared at her for a full-on thirty seconds, unable to believe she had the sheer gall to propose such an idea after tangling him and his two innocent children in this unholy mess.

The safe, comfortable world he wanted for Miriam and Charlie after all they had been through seemed a distant mirage now, thanks to Jane Withington, and now she wanted him to help her escape the justice she deserved.

He would have laughed in her face if he wasn't battling a deep sense of hurt and betrayal.

"Now why would I possibly want to help you escape?" he asked.

She took a shaky breath at his bluntness. "I don't know.

For some silly reason, I thought perhaps you wouldn't want to see me tortured and killed by vicious terrorists. I must have been mistaken."

"You were."

She flinched as if he'd sucker-punched her. Her hand tightened on the railing and her body braced as if expecting another blow.

"I see," she murmured. "And what if I were to take off right now and try to escape on my own before the FBI agents arrived?"

"You can bet I would stop you before you made it very far."

She digested this, her knuckles white on the railing. "I thought Army Rangers were supposed to be all about protecting the helpless and the innocent."

"They are. And if I thought for a minute you were helpless *or* innocent, I might reconsider. But then, since I haven't been an army Ranger for a long time, I guess those rules don't apply, anyway."

She frowned. "But I thought…"

"You picked the wrong man to mess with, Jane. I've spent the last dozen years wallowing in the filth and muck of the world, hunting down people like you and your terrorist cell."

She closed her eyes—in frustration or guilt, he didn't know. "I don't *have* a terrorist cell! Why on earth would I? I'm a translator from Buckinghamshire!"

"Who happens to speak Tagalog, Vandish, Parsi and Arabic. I can think of at least a dozen terrorist organizations who would find great use for someone of your linguistic abilities."

"Provided I agreed to cooperate with them, which I never would!"

She certainly sounded convincing. Her eyes sparked with outraged innocence and sometime in the last few minutes the color had returned to flare high and pink on her cheekbones. Another man probably would have been completely taken in.

Too bad he'd learned early not to trust anyone.

"That's good, sweetheart. That outraged-innocent act should play well with the FBI."

Fear skittered across her features but she quickly contained it. "Are you army intelligence or CIA?" she asked softly after a moment.

"Neither. I'm officially retired."

"Which were you?"

"It doesn't matter. That chapter of my life has been closed."

"You're a spy." She shook her head, an odd expression in her eyes. "I should have known."

"What's that supposed to mean?"

"Nothing." She gazed up at the mountains, just beginning to turn purple with the sunset. "What will you do with me?"

"I don't have anything to do with this. For now we're going to go inside and wait until our friends from the FBI arrive and then I'll wash my hands of you and go back to my life."

"You're making a terrible mistake. Is there anything at all I can say to convince you of that?" Her voice sounded sorrowful, almost without hope, which gave him pause. What if she was telling the truth? What if she had been caught up in this whole thing entirely by bad luck and circumstance?

Yeah, and those mountains might suddenly crumble into dust. He couldn't afford to weaken, not with so much on the line.

She might look the picture of innocence in her borrowed T-shirt and jeans, but it was all an act. He couldn't let himself forget that—though it might be a good idea right about now to develop a little selective amnesia himself and try to forget the soft tenderness he had started to feel for this woman.

She had played him, that was all. Whatever he thought might have been between them had been as much a chimera as the rest of it. She had played him for a fool and he had let her.

"Save your lies for the FBI," he snapped, angry at his weakness. He was even more angry when it took every ounce of self-control to keep his hands tightly fisted at his side so he didn't reach for her when she flinched at his harsh words.

"I'll do that, then," she murmured, her eyes on a dark spot on the horizon.

A car, he realized, traveling up the long Bittercreek driveway. If he wasn't mistaken, it looked like the kind of bland dark sedan favored by the unimaginative FBI.

He had time only for one quick flash of annoyance at Cale for not giving him the extra time he had sought, then he realized this way was better. He wanted this done, wanted her out of his life so he could figure out how to go on from here.

"Looks like there's your ride."

She was breathing rapidly, shallowly, he realized, and her pupils were wide with panic and desperation.

She clutched his arm, her gaze glued on the sedan as it made its inexorable way toward them. "Mason, please! You can't let them take me. You saved me once. Can't you do it again?"

What new game was this? "I don't know what you're talking about. I didn't save you from anything."

"Yes, you did." She sucked in a huge gulp of air. "You *did*. The moment the fog in my mind lifted this morning, I remembered you. You were there, part of the rescue team in Colombia when my father died. I wanted to run back to help him and you wouldn't let me. You grabbed me and tossed me into a helicopter. I would have died just like Harry if you hadn't. I've never forgotten you. Well, except for the last few days."

Suddenly everything clicked. He realized exactly why she had looked so vaguely familiar to him and why her name had struck a chord somewhere deep inside him the moment Cale mentioned it.

"Harry Withington was your father. You're that girl we rescued from that FARC rebel camp."

"Yes!"

He'd all but forgotten that incident because of the hundreds that had come later. He had been a young soldier, still idealistic, still caught up in the Ranger's "We Lead the Way" mentality.

He had a vague memory of a half-starved wraith of a girl sobbing on his shoulder all the way to Bogota, where his unit had been having training exercises with the Colombian military when they had been activated for a rescue.

He hadn't thought of her in years but now he wondered that he had missed the connection.

"I would never associate with people who want to rule by terror, Mason." She spoke quickly, urgently, as the government sedan came within fifty yards. "I *couldn't!* I know firsthand what they're capable of. I know what it's like to spend six days in a hole in the ground, afraid every moment would be my last. I saw my father die right in front of my eyes. *You* saw him die. All I ever wanted after that terrible experience was a comfortable, safe life. You must believe me!"

How much more complicated could this all get? Just when he had steeled himself against her, she tossed a grenade like this at him. He remembered that girl, remembered that chopper ride and how he had held her while she screamed and sobbed for her father.

Near the end of the ride she had collapsed from grief, exhaustion and hunger, and finally slept but he had been reluctant to release her. Later his team members rode him mercilessly about it, but he had held tight until they landed at the air base outside Bogota, when he had turned her over to waiting embassy officials.

The experience had affected him profoundly, one of several that swayed him to accept the agency's offer when they came calling not long after.

Could someone who had been through such a hideous ordeal at the hands of rebels—little more than terrorists and bullies—align herself with men of similar ilk?

He had a tough time believing it. On the other hand, Cale said the case against her was airtight.

What a tangled mess. He didn't know what the hell to do. He had learned to rely on his instincts over the years but those instincts hadn't exactly been reliable the last few days.

Right now he didn't trust himself to be rational about Jane Withington. He wanted to believe her story, not just because of the brief intersection of their respective pasts but because he hated thinking those instincts had gone so haywire.

But if he was wrong, he would be letting a terrorist escape justice. He couldn't risk it—and he couldn't risk any further threat to his children's safety or security. If he helped her escape, *he* would be the one going into FBI custody. And then what would happen to Miriam and Charlie?

"If you haven't done anything wrong, you don't have to worry. It will all sort itself out."

"You can't honestly believe that, can you?"

He felt a qualm of guilt but forced himself to think of Charlie and Miriam. "I can't help you, Jane."

A tiny light flickered out in her gaze and she seemed to withdraw inside herself. "Won't, you mean."

"Can't," he repeated.

She gripped the railing, looking fragile and frightened. In her borrowed teenager clothes, she looked as young as that frightened fifteen-year-old yanked out of a hole in Colombia and he wondered again how he had possibly missed the resemblance.

The sedan finally reached the house and two men climbed out. When they were still out of earshot, Jane turned to him, her voice so low he could barely hear it.

"I used to dream about you. My knight in battle armor. As a fifteen-year-old girl, I fell a little in love with the handsome American soldier who rescued me. I didn't know your name but you were everything good and decent in the world to me."

She drew in a shaky breath. "As I spent today with you and the children, I thought I was falling in love with you all over again. But I must have been mistaken. How could I be in love with someone like you? You're just a hard, empty shell, with nothing inside you but mistrust and suspicion."

Her words cut into him like whirling machetes. Before he could begin to think of an answer, the two men reached the porch.

"Ms. Withington?" The younger agent who spoke could have been the FBI poster boy, with his crew cut and pleasant features. Mason was stunned by his desire to beat the crap out of him. "We're agents with the Federal Bureau of Investigation. Would you come with us, please?"

She looked defeated, completely worn down. Confused and aching, Mason stepped forward, enough hero left in him to try to protect her as much as possible. "IDs?"

The agents both gave him the once-over, then presented their identification. He studied them carefully then handed them back.

"They're legit. Just go with them, Jane. I still have contacts in intelligence circles. I'll make sure you're given extra protection in custody and that you're treated fairly."

She lifted blue eyes to his and he was stunned by the lack of expression in them before she allowed the FBI agents to lead her into their sedan, put her in the back seat and close the door behind her.

He watched the agents climb in, then start the sedan and take off down the driveway, wondering if he had just made the biggest mistake of his life.

An empty shell of a man, she had called him. She couldn't have been more wrong. A man who couldn't feel would not have to suffer this pain and wrenching guilt as he watched the dark sedan's taillights disappear over the rise.

He stood and watched until he couldn't even see a cloud of dust from the vehicle, then he opened the door, to be met instantly by the children.

"We saw a car. Where is Jane? Who are the men?" Miriam asked.

How did he explain all of this to the children? Easy. He

couldn't. "Um, she had to go away." That much was true, at least.

Miriam appeared to digest this. "When will she return?"

He should prevaricate—he was damn good at it, after all—but somehow he couldn't force out a convenient lie. Instead, he gripped Miriam's little hands in his. "I don't know if she will, honey. I'm sorry."

She gazed up at him in disbelief for nearly a full moment, then her face crumpled and she started to cry. Her tears broke his heart, especially since she usually held her pain deep inside herself.

"She did not say goodbye. She was my friend. Why did she did not say goodbye?"

He pulled her into his arms, completely out of his depth with a young crying female. It didn't help that his own throat felt gritty, clogged with emotion. Charlie started to cry, too, more in sympathy with his sister, Mason thought, but it didn't make his tears any less real.

"Why did she go?" Miriam wailed.

He didn't have the first idea how to respond to that. Before he could come up with an adequate answer, his cell phone buzzed in his pocket. He wanted to ignore it but a quick glance at the caller ID identified the caller as Cale Davis.

"Yeah?" he said shortly. He wanted to be angry with Cale for sending the agents out earlier than he expected but couldn't manage to summon anything but pain. He couldn't blame the other man. Not really. He was just doing his job, trying to make the case. Mason had certainly been in his shoes a time or two.

Besides, it was probably better not to delay the inevitable, anyway. Sooner begun, sooner done, his mother used to say.

"Just wanted to let you know two agents are on their way to pick up your Brit."

Not his Brit, he thought. Not anymore. "They've come and gone. She's on her way in."

Cale said nothing for several seconds, just long enough to make Mason itchy all over again. "What do you mean, on her way? That's impossible. I just talked to my agents before I called you and they're still fifteen or twenty minutes out."

Chapter 15

At the FBI agent's words, Mason's heart seemed to stutter to a stop.

He drew in a deep breath, his hand fisted around the phone. "There must be some kind of mix-up. Two of your agents picked her up ten minutes ago."

"They weren't ours. I swear it."

Shit. Shit, shit, *shit!*

She was right! He should have listened to her. She had been afraid for her safety, had tried to tell him, and he had handed her over to certain death.

Fear clutched at his insides with cold, bony fingers. He couldn't seem to make his brain work beyond having the presence of mind to slip away from the children to his office down the hall.

He closed the door behind him and leaned against it, fighting the panic in his chest.

"They had proper credentials, Cale. I checked them my-self. They were legit."

Even as he said the words, he mentally groaned. He knew as well as Cale that FBI credentials could be manu-factured. Hell, he'd had some himself at one time, as well as a half-dozen passports with different names and nation-alities. Even if they were legitimate, Jane had tried to tell him Djami had FBI agents on the payroll.

The minute Cale told his superiors he knew where to find Jane Withington, the call could have gone out to Djami. His men could have gotten a headstart on the legit-imate agents.

What an idiot. He had been so busy trying to deal with his anger and hurt, his deep sense of betrayal, that he never dared believe for a moment that Jane could have been tell-ing the truth.

What had he done? Those icy fingers clawed tighter.

"Maybe there are members of the VLF cell still at large who engineered some kind of an escape," Cale suggested.

Mason found the suggestion completely absurd and in that moment, the truth slammed into him with the force of a freight train.

Jane Withington couldn't be a terrorist, any more than he was. He had come to know her these last few days and he had been stupid to believe for one second that a woman who could be so gentle and loving to his children would be willing to detonate a bomb that would likely kill hundreds.

He *had* believed it, though. Why? Maybe she was right. Maybe he had nothing left inside him but doubt and suspicion.

He had been in the game so long he saw enemy com-batants everywhere he looked.

How could I be in love with someone like you? You're just a hard, empty shell, with nothing inside you but mistrust and suspicion.

"No. This has all been a diversion," he said, his heart aching. "She's not VLF. I'd stake my life on it."

He might have to.

With the phone still pressed to his ear, he raced up the stairs. "Look, I need your help. I'm out of the loop and I need information," he said to Cale as he worked the combination safe and pulled out his Ruger and extra ammo.

"Let me make a few calls to try to figure out what's going on and I'll get back to you," Cale said.

He didn't have that long to wait. "Can you get me everything you know on Simon Djami, the Vandelusian trade minister, especially where the hell he is right now?"

Cale's confusion came through loud and clear on the phone. "You think she's going after Djami? Could he have been the target of the planned attack all along?"

"I think he's the leader of the VLF. She tried to tell me and I wouldn't listen and now he has her."

"I thought you said FBI agents picked her up."

"I can't explain right now. You're just going to have to trust me."

"Djami has been all over the news this week praising the treaty process. He's the frigging Vandelusian trade minister!"

"He's also the one who ordered Jane killed when she overheard him and his cell ironing out final details of the bombing."

Cale's pause was pregnant with doubt. "You know how far-fetched that sounds?" he finally asked.

"If you knew her, you would see it's even more far-fetched to believe her capable of working with the VLF.

She survived a terrorist kidnapping when she was fifteen and she watched her father die during her rescue."

"Listen to yourself, man. You're too close to this. You'll believe any wild story she tells you. You need to step back and let us handle things."

"It's not a wild story. I was there, damn you. I was one of the American soldiers who pulled her out of the hole they kept her in for six days. I threw her in the chopper and practically had to sit on her so she wouldn't run back to her father and suffer the same fate he did. She is not involved in this, Cale. She knows Djami is involved with the VLF and he's already tried to kill her once because of that knowledge. If I don't hurry, he's going to try again. I just need to know where Djami's staying during the summit."

"You can't just storm the place and drag her back out."

Just watch me, he thought, shoving his clutch piece into his boot.

"Where is he?"

Cale sighed. "You aren't content torching your own career, now you want to watch mine crash and burn, too?"

"Forget it. I'll find out on my own."

He was just getting ready to sever the connection when Cale stopped him. "Wait. Give me a minute and I'll do what I can."

"Just call me back."

He severed the connection and raced back down the stairs, trying to calculate how quickly he could get to Park City, taking into account that he would have to drop the kids with Pam.

In the kitchen, he found the children huddled together. Miriam's face was streaked with tears and she looked frightened.

"What is happening?" she asked. "Jane, she is okay?"

He pulled both of them into his arms, hating that this kind of ugliness had touched them again.

"Jane's going to be just fine. But I need you and Charlie to stay with Pam for a while, okay? I'm going to drop you off at her house while I take care of some business."

"Will you bring Jane back?"

"Oh, honey. I'm going to do my best."

"Would you mind telling me where you're taking me?"

She might as well be talking to the ceiling, for all the notice the two men in the front seat gave her. This was the third time she had tried to engage them in conversation and each time they ignored her as if she were nothing more than a package to be delivered.

She had to admit, she found their total lack of acknowledgement more terrifying than if they had treated her to threats and intimidation. At least then she would have had something concrete to fear.

This vague, amorphous dread made her want to cower in the back seat, to curl into the fetal position and pretend none of this was happening. She hated being afraid—and she hated more that she had no idea what to do with her fear.

Courage, Janie-girl.

Harry's voice sounded in her head again—and if he'd actually been there instead of a being a figment of her overheated imagination, she would have liked to box his ears.

Where the devil had he been for three days while she'd been rusticating at the Bittercreek ranch with Mason and the children? She certainly could have used a little paternal advice to caution her against tumbling in love with someone completely inappropriate.

She was in love with a spy, someone so like her father it would have been laughable if she didn't find it so terribly sad. While she might have nurtured a soft place in her heart for the handsome American soldier who had helped rescue her from her kidnappers, she had been smart enough even at fifteen to know he was only the kind of man for dreams, not reality.

She had seen what her mother went through every time Harry popped in for his rare visits and then popped out again on his way to save the world. Oh, Harry had ostensibly been in Her Majesty's diplomatic corps, but in his case that had simply been a front for some of his more clandestine activities. He'd never told her about any of them but she had known, even before her mother died, and Jane had joined his world.

When Harry wasn't there, all the light would go out of Claire. She would jump every time the phone rang and panic every time a stranger knocked on the door.

Not for Jane. A kind, quiet man. That's the type she needed. Not a hard, dangerous man with ice in his veins.

Harry probably would have adored Mason. She frowned at the thought even as she acknowledged the truth of it. Harry would have slapped him on the back, handed him a pint and pulled up a chair so they could have a nice chat about the places they had both seen, the people they had known, the things they had done.

And she had to admit that Mason didn't exactly fit her father's mold. When her mother had died, Harry had simply collected her from Buckinghamshire and dragged her along with him, without allowing her presence to appreciably change his life in the slightest.

Mason, on the other hand, had returned to his family's

ranch with Charlie and Miriam to make a new home for them. Had he quit the spy business then?

He must have, if he was devoting his energies to the breeding and training of horses, but she would probably never have the chance to ask him. She shivered and swallowed her frightened sob just before it sneaked free.

For all she knew, these could indeed be FBI agents, she reminded herself, transporting her to whatever holding facility they might take suspected terrorists.

She had to cling to a little hope, anyway, though she found it quite frightening that she found jail the best scenario she could come up with.

It was a hollow hope, she had to admit. With every passing mile, the days she spent with Mason and the children seemed from another world.

She hated that her last words to him had been cruel and cutting, and she suddenly would have given anything to take them back. He didn't deserve her animosity.

How could she blame him for not helping her escape? He would be risking everything for someone he had only known for a few days and he had two children to think about. Two sweet, wonderful children Jane dearly wanted to see once more, to at least kiss goodbye before she returned to England and her colorless life.

Of course, right now, England and that colorless life seemed an impossible dream.

Courage. You can get out of this mess as you've done the others.

She glared as Harry's hearty voice sounded in her ears again. Unless you have something a little more helpful to offer, stick a sock in it, she muttered to her imagination, and could swear she heard chuckling.

This unrelenting terror was turning her into a certified nutcase. She let out a breath and straightened her shoulders. *Charlie and Miriam.* Thinking of them would give her courage.

"Excuse me," she said in a voice surely pitched too loud for the men in the front seat to ignore. "I really must insist you tell me where you're taking me."

She thought for a moment they would ignore her but then the man in the passenger seat—older than the other by perhaps a decade, with salt-and-pepper hair and blue eyes that seemed to bore through skin and bones—turned toward her.

"For questioning," he answered, then turned around again.

"Can you tell me where?"

Apparently that was an answer she was doomed to discover only when they arrived at their destination because he turned back around and said nothing.

Really, these men could take her anywhere, do anything to her, and no one would know. Mason was the only person who knew she had been taken into custody by two men claiming to be FBI agents.

She could only hope that if she turned up missing, he would be interested enough in the woman who had lived in his house for three days to investigate what might have happened to her.

She clutched her fingers tightly in her lap and watched the passing scenery. In only a few moments they took an exit off the thoroughfare and she started to recognize the resort town of Park City.

Would the FBI have offices here? she wondered but she couldn't begin to guess.

Like many ski resorts in the West, Park City had started

life as a mining town, wild and raucous, she had learned in her two days in town before that fateful restaurant encounter. In the Old Town area, the streets were steep and narrow, and that was the direction the two FBI agents took.

With every passing moment as they left the stores and restaurants behind, her hope that they were taking her to some kind of holding area dissipated. This area appeared residential, with large vacation homes mostly built of logs, their outside walls decorated with skis and snowshoes and other outdoorsy icons.

Where were they going?

At last, when her tension had reached fever pitch, the younger agent pulled the automobile to a stop in front of a massive log-and-stone structure with soaring windows in front and a series of steeply pitched gables.

They pulled open the door and waited for her. She had one wild rebellious moment where she wondered what they would do if she stayed where she was. Would they yank her out of the automobile, kicking and screaming, and drag her into the house?

She could always take off running. The idea flitted across her mind. Would they dare shoot her in a residential area at the time of day when families were coming home to dinner?

Maybe not, but they would no doubt catch her. She had never been much of an athlete, and the younger agent, at least, looked in prime physical condition.

She sighed, wondering when Harry Withington's little girl would ever get a spine.

One of the agents made an impatient sound and Jane unfolded tight muscles and slid from the car.

The flanked her as they walked up wide steps and into

the house, after punching a code in a box cleverly concealed by a false rock in the facade.

The interior was decorated in an American-West style—Navajo blankets on the wall, a chandelier fashioned of entwined antlers, even a mounted buffalo head above a stone fireplace. Under other circumstances, she might have enjoyed its rustic elegance, but she could scarcely breathe with the nerves scrambling through her.

The house appeared empty—at least no one came out to greet them. She wasn't sure whether to take that as a good sign.

Her armed escorts ushered her into a small chamber off the main gathering room, still without saying anything to her. The room had no windows and only the single door, though it was comfortably appointed.

She was tired and hungry and scared and she needed to use the loo but she decided she would rather burst then have to ask these men directions.

Not that they gave her much chance to ask anything. They all but shoved her into the room and slammed the door behind her. An instant later she heard a lock click.

She was well and truly trapped.

"Now what, Harry?" she said aloud, but her capricious father didn't answer this time. Maybe he expected her to get herself out. Or maybe he had finally given up on his chicken-livered offspring.

"I'm sorry I've been a disappointment to you," she said softly. "I'm weak and cowardly. Afraid to die but more terrified to live. You're partly to blame, you know. I was never like you. I just wasn't."

As she spoke aloud to the father who could no longer hear her—and who never listened even when he could—

she wandered the room, looking in vain for something she might use as a weapon. There were no lamps, no handy fireplace pokers. Nothing but a massive carved chest in the corner that no amount of effort could unlock.

"I tried to be brave because I loved you and wanted to be with you, but I hated our life," she went on, gritting her teeth as she tried without success to pry the lock. "You should have seen that, Harry. If you had, I might not have grown up in hotel rooms with angry crowds out on the streets and the sound of distant gunfire to put me to sleep at night. That was no way to raise a child. Mason has it right. Children need peace and safety, room to stretch and grow, to spread out roots."

If she'd had that, what kind of woman might she have become? she wondered.

"Strong and beautiful, just as you are now," her father's voice whispered in her head.

Ah, so *there* was the proof that that voice was just a figment of her imagination: she was strong and beautiful only in her deepest dreams.

Before she could answer, she heard a key in the lock, then the door swung open.

Panic fluttered through her on wild wings. She caught her breath, then turned toward the door, dreading who she would find there.

Mason had just reached the foothills of Park City when his cell phone finally rang.

He picked it up and saw the caller was Cale. "Where am I going?" he asked.

"Guantanamo, if you're wrong about this," the FBI agent growled.

"I'm not wrong. I can feel it in my gut. Djami has her. I know it."

"And you think he's just going to hand her over to you for the hell of it?"

Not without a fight, but Mason was prepared to give the bastard one.

"Where is he staying?"

"The man likes his privacy, I'll give him that much. It took some arm-twisting but I finally have an address. He's rented an entire block of vacation homes in the Deer Valley area for him and his staff."

"Just tell me where."

Cale gave him the address and Mason pulled over just long enough to punch it into his truck's navigation system. A detailed map flashed on the small screen.

"I've got it. Thanks. I owe you."

"You're not going on your own, Keller. One of the reasons I took so long was so I could dig around into Djami's background a little."

"And?"

"He's got a sterling record on the surface. Forward-thinking, very pro-West. An ideal trade minister. But if you go down a few levels, the picture gets a little more complicated, a little more shaded. Djami has more than a few acquaintances on several countries' watch lists and his reported income doesn't quite match his lifestyle."

"What else?" Mason knew those few details might be enough to launch an investigation but not the kind of raid that would be needed to rescue Jane in time.

"An hour ago, fishermen at Jordanelle Reservoir pulled out the decomposing body of a man who appears to be of Southeast Asian descent. The man had no identification on him but he did have a slip of paper in his pocket with a single phone number—which, if you happened to dial, would connect you to Simon Djami's cell phone."

"Still flimsy."

"Patriot Act, man. Doesn't take much for a search warrant when you're talking suspected terrorism. The Homeland Security team is preparing to serve the search warrant within the hour."

"I can't wait that long. She could be dead in an hour!"

Cale was silent for maybe ten seconds. When he spoke, his voice was compassionate and Mason realized how much he must have revealed through his outburst.

"I'm sorry, Mason," the FBI agent said quietly. "It's the best I can do right now."

Mason drew in a breath and ordered himself to maintain. "I know. I appreciate the address."

"Don't do anything crazy. It's going to be hard enough to explain how you obtained that information."

"Don't worry. I'll keep you out of it."

"You know that's not what I'm concerned about. Be careful."

Mason made some noncommittal sound and ended the call, then put his truck back in gear and started driving.

Jane had perhaps five seconds for sheer, unadulterated fear to jab at her before Simon Djami walked into the room in the brilliant white, flowing ceremonial robes she remembered from her time in Vandelusia. Two other men who looked Vandish joined him and stood just inside the door. They were short, probably no taller than she, but heavily muscled and she thought she saw ominous bulges under their suit jackets.

With a grim sense of inevitability, she watched Djami move closer. She had known it would come to this. Oh, she might have tried to cling to some foolish hope about the FBI, but in her heart she had always known what awaited her.

He stopped five feet away from her and studied her out of intense dark eyes for a long drawn-out moment, until she began to squirm, feeling underdressed and rather exposed in her borrowed clothes, the low-cut jeans and the brilliant T-shirt. She would have given anything right then for the psychological armor of one of her boring, conservative business suits.

"Ms. Withington," he said in Vandish. "I am afraid you have caused me a great deal of trouble."

For an instant, part of her urged obsequiousness—to grovel, to bow and scrape and apologize for having the effrontery to inconvenience him. She let out a breath. No. It wouldn't make a difference to this cold, conscienceless man and would leave her debased and humiliated.

She had lived a coward. She wasn't prepared to die one.

"Good," she answered in English, hoping the smirk she pasted on her lips came through for all the trembling.

His eyes darkened and he raised an arm. She thought he might strike her but instead he gestured to one of his henchmen, who stepped forward and without even blinking, slapped her with the back of his hand so hard it knocked her to the floor.

She gasped in pain and surprise, tears burning her eyes. She blinked hard to force them back and dropped her hand from the terrible ache in her cheek, unwilling to give these brutal men the satisfaction of knowing they had hurt her.

With a wary eye toward the thug who had struck her,

she climbed to her knees then rose to her feet, praying her unsteady legs would hold her.

The man with the mean backhand looked at his boss with a question in his eyes but Djami shook his head.

When he spoke, Jane found his voice the more chilling for its complete control, with no trace of the fury she could see in his eyes. "You are one stupid woman. One insignificant whore. Look at you, with your infidel clothes and your uncovered hair. You are nothing. You should have been a minor inconvenience. How have you managed single-handedly to destroy something that has been months in the planning?"

"Sheer dumb luck?" She lifted her chin, bracing for another blow, but it didn't come. Instead he laughed, a chilling sound that crawled down her spine like a nasty furry spider.

"Indeed. Indeed."

He circled her, studying her from all angles. She forced herself to remain perfectly still, chin lifted and her back perfectly straight, even though she wanted to huddle into a ball and disappear into the carpet.

"The question now is, what am I to do with you?" Djami asked.

She thought of Harry's insouciance, his complete aplomb in all circumstances. *This one's for you, Daddy.*

"You could always let me go," she suggested.

He laughed again and Jane could swear she now had a dozen spiders crawling up and down her vertebrae.

"Oh, I think not. I'm afraid you're rather more than an inconvenience now."

Chapter 16

Jane didn't know how to respond to that so she decided to keep her mouth shut.

"You see," Djami went on, "I have worked very hard to maintain secrecy around my efforts to see Vandelusia shed western influence and return to her glorious past. I am viewed as a friend to your country and to the United States. I have a position of trust and responsibility and therefore have a unique opportunity to foment change. Should my connection to certain rebel groups become widely known, those opportunities would be in jeopardy."

"Yes. I can see why some in your country and mine might take exception to your involvement with vicious terrorists."

His smile froze her insides another degree. "Just so. Which is why I must ask if you told anyone what you heard in that restaurant."

She thought of Mason and their last bitter scene and her heart ached.

"No," she said flatly. "I told no one."

"I don't believe you."

She tried for a nonchalant shrug, though she was afraid it fell somewhat short. "Who would I possibly tell?"

Djami gestured to the other blank-faced thug. She braced herself, her insides cramping with fear. He didn't hit her, though, he only jerked her arms behind her back and bound them with what felt like one of those plastic handcuffs she had seen police use on the telly.

Not a good sign, she thought, digging deep for the last shreds of composure.

"Three days ago my men were to take you into the mountains and handle the situation."

"Kill me, you mean."

"As you will. Nevertheless, you escaped from them. You must have had help. My associates tell me you have been staying with an American cowboy. It is only a matter of time before we know all there is to know about this man. I must ask you, what have you told him about me?"

She couldn't breathe past her fear suddenly. What had she done? She had put Mason and the children in such terrible danger, and the worst part was she had no way to caution him to beware. If only he had believed her, just a little, he might have some forewarning and could protect those two dear children.

She could only pray that he would find some tiny part of his heart that doubted she could be involved with a bloodthirsty group like the VLF.

"What have you told him?" Djami asked again.

"Nothing! I swear!"

He gestured to Thug Number One, who hit her—harder this time. Again the force of the blow sent her to the ground but this time she had no way to break her fall, with her arms bound behind her back. She landed on her shoulder with a jarring crack and icy pain radiated through her body.

Her vision grayed and she thought she might pass out as the metallic taste of blood filled her mouth. It took all her concentration to stay conscious when all she wanted was to curl into a ball and just let them kill her.

Sobs shook her chest but she forced them down and willed oxygen back into her lungs. She wasn't cut out for this! Breathing ragged, she struggled to rise—the task a hundred times more difficult with her hands bound.

Djami watched her struggle, his features impassive but his eyes ablaze. "You defile my presence with your lies," he said when she reached her feet once more.

She lifted her chin. "You could always leave," she suggested through a mouthful of blood, then could have bitten through the rest of her tongue. Of all the times for her to start channeling Harry!

Mr. Nasty Backhand stepped forward again, his arm upraised, but Djami stopped him.

"What did you tell your American cowboy?"

"Nothing," she repeated. "I had nothing to tell him. While I was trying to escape your men I suffered a head injury that affected my memory. I didn't remember anything about Vandelusia or you or your plans for a terrorist attack at the treaty signing until this morning. I swear I haven't said anything to anyone."

"You might as well tell me. Your lies will not save this man."

No matter what she said or did here, Mason and the children would still be in danger. The realization filled her with dread, with a horrible, nauseating guilt.

Hang on. Be strong, Harry's voice whispered.

You're not helping, she thought furiously, but in some strange way just imagining what he might say if he were here helped calm her, helped her mind force through the panic.

"You know, you can't go around indiscriminately killing people in America without someone sitting up and taking notice," she said.

Djami shrugged. "I will be gone from this cursed land by the time anyone finds you or your cowboy."

The only possible chance she had of protecting Mason and the children was to put Djami on the defensive, she thought, to convince him he didn't have time to worry about any more loose ends if he wanted to save his own neck.

If what she was considering worked, any window of opportunity for escape would close with a bang. But that window was so tiny she doubted she would have been about to drag herself through it, anyway. If he believed her, he would turn his wrath on her all that much more quickly, but she had no choice.

She pictured Mason's face, handsome and hard with those shadows in his eyes, then the children—sweet Miriam, so wise and so sad, and Charlie, a little bundle of energy with such love to give.

Her heart cracked apart knowing she would never see them again.

Was this what Harry had lived through in those precious few seconds as he pushed her ahead of him toward the waiting helicopter and created a diversion, sacrificing himself so his daughter could survive?

Impossibly, she thought she felt the lightest comforting

touch on her throbbing shoulder. It strengthened her, bolstered her.

"You can kill me," she said quietly, "but you won't have the chance to kill the man I stayed with. I can promise you that. You will be in U.S. custody by then. I'm sure I don't need to tell you that this country and my own do not treat terrorists kindly."

The rage in his eyes dimmed a little and she thought she saw unease creep in. "I have diplomatic immunity."

"Not when you plan to kill innocent people."

"Innocent!" The word dripped from his tongue, full of derision. "No one in this country is innocent. They are all godless whoremongers, every single one."

She lifted her chin. "Well, those godless whoremongers are going to fry your testicles, Minister Djami."

At her words, the rage in his eyes rekindled, stronger than ever. "What have you told him?" His voice shook with fury.

"Everything. I told him everything I heard that night, I told him your name, I told him everything. It won't do you any good to kill him. It so happens that American cowboy you speak of with such derision is a U.S. counterintelligence agent."

"You lie!"

She was getting to him—she could see it in his accelerated breathing and clenched fists.

"Not this time. Word is out, Djami. As your FBI lapdogs were driving me away, my cowboy was calling his contacts to share all the information he knew about you. I assure you they will take him quite seriously. If I were you, I would settle in for a long stay here in the States. I don't think you'll be going anywhere, as your passport and your diplomatic immunity status are both no doubt being revoked even as we speak."

Without warning, he struck out himself, the blow whipping her head back. By some miracle she managed to keep her feet this time, though her battered face felt as if it were swelling like a puffer fish.

He came after her again but managed to stop just before making contact. With a shuddering breath, he visibly controlled himself.

"You are resourceful. But then, so am I. After you escaped from my men, I anticipated you would be foolish enough to tell someone what you heard us planning. I made sure no one will believe you—who would trust the word of the woman who planned to carry an explosive device into a historic treaty signing? No one. You are a terrorist and a traitor."

Ah, so this was why Mason thought she was involved with the VLF. Djami had framed her and Mason had bought it.

"Clever."

"Yes. I thought so."

"Only one minor flaw in your plan. No one who has met me would ever attribute to me the courage to carry out something like that. I'm a coward, Mr. Djami, and everyone knows it."

"Perhaps the little mouse hides a warrior's heart. You are brave enough to taunt me now. Foolish. Very, very foolish, but the brave often are."

He shrugged. "The evidence I left against you is without question. When you disappear, those who are looking for you will assume you fled the country to avoid justice. You will be reviled and hated, Ms. Withington."

He offered a particularly abhorrent smile that chilled her more than anything else in this miserable little drama. "Of course, all that won't matter to you since you will be dead."

She held her breath and Djami left her and walked to the chest she had seen when she had been thrown in the room. He pulled a key from his robes and handed it to Ugly Thug Number Two, who unlocked the chest and threw open the lid.

From the depths of it, Djami pulled out a large machete-type weapon she recognized as having the curved shape and intricate carving of a Vandelusian ceremonial *jagpang* with its wickedly sharp blade.

She imagined that blade cutting through skin, and the room started to spin.

Breathe! she ordered herself. *Think!* She tried, but the sight of that *jagpang* shoved every other rational thought from her mind.

The two thugs moved to her side and held her fast as Djami advanced, holding the weapon as if it were a favorite pet.

"Yes, Ms. Withington. I am afraid you have been a great deal more than an inconvenience," Djami said. "And now you will pay the price for the trouble you have caused."

The two men tried to force her down and she started to hyperventilate. No! She would not go quietly. She fought them, kicking out and trying to break free but they were stronger than she. One wrenched her injured shoulder with beefy hands and she was unable to hold back one raw, ragged cry of fear and pain as they shoved her to her knees.

Mason studied the map on his navigation system. He was close—one more turn and he would be on the right street. His nerves were stretched tight and adrenaline pumped through him. He had to be in time. He refused to consider any other alternative.

Just as he reached the intersection, a vehicle approached him on his left, from the direction of Djami's house. It was a dark blue sedan, he realized. The men who had taken Jane from the Bittercreek! Instead of turning, he drove straight through the intersection, shifting his face as he passed the sedan so they wouldn't recognize him, though he thought he was moderately safe as his pickup truck was high enough off the ground they wouldn't have a clear field of sight.

He drove slowly through the residential area until he saw the sedan turn and head down the hill to the city center.

She was here. Seeing that sedan confirmed it. As he pulled into a driveway and turned the truck around to head in the right direction, he didn't know whether to be relieved or even more nervous.

Remembering that Cale said Djami had rented the entire street, he decided on a stealth approach. He parked his truck on the next block and made his way through two backyards until he came out onto Aspen Ridge Road.

Djami's rented quarters were in a huge log home with wide steps leading to a rock porch that covered half of the house. Thick shrubs grew against the logs on the other half and extended across the front of the porch. Not the best landscaping for the security-conscious but certainly convenient for surveillance.

It was an easy matter to slip into the shrubs for a clear view through the front window.

When he straightened, he saw he had just missed being discovered by a lone guard patrolling the massive great room of the house. The man looked Vandish and cradled an assault weapon that appeared to be Russian-made.

Frozen in place, Mason watched for several long moments as the guard traveled the perimeter of the room, pausing at the windows to look out. The guard started to head off down a long hallway and Mason decided he needed to act before he moved too far out of earshot.

He climbed up to the porch and scratched softly on the door, then slid back into the bushes, crouching down below the level of the porch. He had no view of the door but he heard it swing open, then a few moments later booted footsteps thudded on the wooden porch as the guard walked out to investigate the mystery sound.

He could hear the man just above him but in full summer the shrubs did an excellent job of concealing him. Someone really ought to let the landlord know what a security risk they were.

A moment later the guard muttered what Mason thought was the Vandish word for *cats* then he heard him turn around and take a step back toward the door.

He waited just a few more seconds, gauging his moment, then vaulted onto the porch silently behind the man. Just before the guard would have made it inside, Mason grabbed him in a choke hold and tapped the butt of his Ruger against the man's temple.

The guard sagged in his arms, immediately unconscious, and Mason quickly relieved him of his assault rifle and rolled him off the porch and into those convenient bushes—out of view of any nosy neighbors.

Or since Djami owned the street temporarily, out of view of any of his comrades who might wander by.

Never had he been more grateful for his training as

he sidled inside, the Russian rifle and his own Ruger at the ready.

He encountered no one else in the great room and he paused for a moment, trying to figure out which direction to go.

Where were they keeping Jane? She had to be here, the only trick was figuring whereabouts, as he judged the house to be at least eight thousand square feet.

Only one thing for it. He was just going to have to start a room-by-room search.

He decided to start upstairs and work his way down, and started to head toward the curving half-log stairs when a high, frightened cry ripped through the house.

"Scream all you like. There is no one to hear you but us."

Part of her would have liked to comply past that first strangled cry and scream the rafters down, but that would have required a little lung capacity on her part and right now as she watched Djami approach with the deadly *jagpang* she couldn't seem to work air through her windpipe.

"No screams?" Djami said with a mocking smile. "Ah, well. You will scream before we are done. I will not make this easy for you. You are an enemy of Vandelusia and you must pay for what you have done. And when I am finished with you, I will find and kill your American cowboy."

She couldn't stop a tiny whimper from escaping as he stepped forward. The guards forced her facedown into the carpet and she suddenly realized with a hideous spurt of bile what Djami meant to do.

Come on, Janie-girl. Keep your head, the voice in her mind said.

Oh, brilliant idea, Harry, she thought hysterically, but once more that voice seemed to steady her.

Behind her, she heard a tiny whir of air as Djami lifted the *jagpang* over his head. The guards stepped back out of his way and she grabbed for that tiny window of opportunity with both hands.

As the blade came down with a sickening whoosh, she had a microsecond to scream again, louder this time, and roll out of the way. They hadn't bothered to bind her legs and she used them now, sweeping out at Djami with all her strength to knock him off his feet.

Panic and survival mode gave her added power and somewhat to her surprise, he toppled backward, cursing at her violently in Vandish as the blade landed harmlessly by the carved trunk.

Now what, Harry?

One guard went to help Djami while the other came after her. He grabbed her and hauled her up and then all hell broke loose.

She heard a rapid-fire pop from the doorway and the guard next to her fell to the ground, still holding her and dragging her down with him.

More gunshots rang out and she found herself in the middle of a raging gunbattle as Djami and the other guard returned fire.

She heard a cry and saw the second guard go down but Djami continued returning fire.

What was happening? Who was there? The light fixture overhead exploded and shards of glass showered around her. With a small, frightened cry, she pulled her legs free of the first downed guard, desperate for cover.

With her arms still bound, she had to slither like a slug

but she finally made it behind the trunk, out of the way of both firing parties, or at least she hoped.

She spied the *jagpang,* still deadly and ominous, and dragged herself to it, desperately raking her bound hands against the blade again and again until she felt the plastic tie fray then give way.

Once free, she turned her attention to determining who might be shooting at them. From here she had a view of the doorway the gunman was firing from. He was concealed around the corner as Djami shot at him, but when he reached around to return fire, she recognized hard, handsome features and intense silver eyes.

Her jaw dropped. "Mason!" she exclaimed, stunned and elated.

He had come for her! She could scarcely believe it.

"Jane, stay down," he ordered and she realized her cry had drawn Djami's attention to her.

His features were contorted with rage now and he started toward her, leaving his cover behind one of the leather sofas.

Mason chose that moment to roll into the room and ended in a low crouch, firing at the trade minister as the man advanced on her. Djami staggered back and Jane saw blood explode through the white of his robes at the right shoulder. She thought he would go down from the injury. Instead, he switched the gun to his left hand and fired at Mason, exposed now in the middle of the room.

She watched, horrified, as the weapon flew from Mason's hands and he fell to his knees then landed facedown on the carpet and went still.

"No!" she screamed. He couldn't be dead. Not after all this. She couldn't bear it.

The horror turned to icy dread as Djami advanced on Mason, the gun pointed at his head.

She couldn't watch. It was too much like that last terrible moment with Harry, watching the rebel leader brutally end his life as she was tossed into the waiting helicopter.

She turned her head and her gaze landed on the *jagpang*. She hadn't been able to help Harry. But damn it, she would not let Djami fire a bullet into Mason's brain.

Praying for strength, driven by grief and rage, she grabbed the weapon and with a violent cry she hefted it over her head and rushed for Djami, heedless of the horrendous pain in her shoulder.

He turned at the sound and fired on her but the shot went wild. In the instant before she would have struck him, another shot rang out and the spot she'd been aiming for was suddenly empty as Djami fell.

Momentum carried her forward and the blade lodged into the leather of the sofa. She sagged after it and stayed there clutching the hilt for a long moment, aware of the awful silence behind her.

She wasn't sure what had happened and she didn't really care. Consumed by a terrible grief, she couldn't seem to move from her spot, kneeling there by the sofa. Let Djami finish the job. Her survival instincts seemed to have abandoned her.

Two men she loved—two wonderful, honorable men—had died trying to save her and she couldn't bear it. First Harry, now Mason. They both should have just let her die—she wasn't worth their sacrifice.

She let out one sobbing breath and screwed her eyes shut, waiting for Djami to kill her. She couldn't bear the idea of having to live with this horrible pain and loss.

"Janie? You still with me?"

"Shut up, Harry," she muttered wearily.

A long silence met her words, then a slightly disgruntled voice asked, "Who the hell is Harry?"

Chapter 17

She frowned. That certainly sounded like Mason's voice. Wonderful. Now she had two dead men in her head.

Behind her she heard rustling and then a grunt. Was Djami coming after her again? She lifted her head and turned slowly, warily. Her fear disappeared in a rush as shock and joy poured over her.

It wasn't Djami moving around—it was Mason! He sat six feet away, pale and pressing a blood-soaked shoulder with a hand that still held a small revolver.

She had never seen a more wonderful sight.

"You're alive!" she exclaimed and launched herself at him. With another grunt, he landed on his rear end.

"For now," he muttered, but his arm slid around her and pulled her tight.

"You came for me. Just like before, you came for me."

Mason had to close his eyes against the guilt and pain.

If he had trusted her in the first place, she never would have been in this situation. He could have protected her, could have concealed her from the men Djami sent for her. She would have been safe at the Bittercreek right now, where she belonged, instead of battered and bleeding in the middle of this gruesome scene.

He would never forget the icy fear in his gut when he had burst through that door and seen her on her knees with Djami's blade poised above her head. All his years of training, both in the Rangers and after, flew out the window and he had acted entirely out of fury. If he'd been thinking, he never would have started firing so indiscriminately.

She easily could have been killed in the crossfire. Another brick of guilt to add to his burden.

"Sorry it took so long," he murmured. He finally had a clear view of her swollen face and in that moment he forgot about the mistakes he'd made. He would have killed Djami all over again if the bastard wasn't already dead. Blood dripped from a cracked lip and her face bore the clear print of a man's hand.

"I should have trusted you," he murmured. "I should have trusted my instincts about you. Should have trusted my heart."

"It doesn't matter. You're here now." She pressed her battered cheek to his and he couldn't seem to breathe around the tenderness soaking through him, filling all the dark and empty places inside him with joy.

He couldn't help himself, he kissed her—a quick, fierce kiss of celebration that they had both survived.

In that moment, he heard voices in the doorway. He barely had time to wrench his mouth away and move in front of Jane, his Ruger in his uninjured hand, before a half dozen men poured into the room, Cale Davis leading the way.

They stood inside the room, surveying the carnage. Djami wasn't moving but both guards had started to moan. Shattered glass and shell casings were everywhere.

"Nothing like leaving a mess for us to clean up," Cale said dryly. "I guess you found her."

Mason let his weapon fall, sick again remembering how he'd found her, kneeling and helpless. "Yeah. Just in time. See that nasty blade embedded in the couch? When I walked into the party, Djami had it poised over her neck. If I'd been thirty seconds later, I would have been too late."

She shuddered against his back and though his shoulder hurt like a son of a bitch, he pulled her back into his arms. He couldn't seem to stop touching her. He wondered if he ever would.

"Ah. That explains a little of the mess. Shoot first, ask questions later?"

"Something like that. Jane Withington, this is Cale Davis, your friendly neighborhood FBI agent."

She stiffened and he remembered she had little reason to trust FBI agents.

"He's one of the good guys," Mason assured her and she relaxed. He had to swallow, amazed that she could trust him so completely after he hadn't had the courage to do the same with her.

Cale smiled. "A pleasure, ma'am."

"I'm counting three tangoes here, one dead and two injured," one of the other agents said.

"Djami?" Mason asked.

Cale shook his head and Mason felt Jane shudder again.

"There's one more in the bushes out front," he said, starting to feel a little woozy.

"Yeah, we found that one. He was just coming around

when we pulled up." Cale grinned. "You're one hell of a fighter, Keller. Are you really sure you're ready to retire?"

He thought of Charlie and Miriam and had a fierce wish to see them, to hold them and make sure they were safe. "Yeah," he murmured, suddenly more exhausted than he'd ever been. "I'm done."

As if from a great distance, he heard Cale make some comment about quitting while he was ahead and going out with a bang. He barely heard him, focusing all his efforts on holding tight to Jane. He couldn't let her go, even though it was taking everything he had.

Hold on.

It was the last thought he had for a while.

His cover was blown and he was being tortured.

They were jabbing needles in his arm, tying him down and blowing poison air into his face.

Jane. He had to save Jane. He started fighting, desperate to be free.

"Easy. You're okay. Easy."

He blinked away the wooziness and found that he was being tortured but it wasn't by any terrorist cell. He was on a stretcher, with medics bustling around him, an IV in his arm and an oxygen mask over his face.

He pulled the thing away, hating that sensation of dry air being forced into his lungs.

"Jane?"

"I'm here." She gripped his left hand.

"What happened?"

"One moment you were with us, the next you weren't."

"I fainted," he said in disgust.

"You passed out," she corrected. "The medics said

you've lost a great deal of blood. They seemed to think it was amazing you made it as long as you did."

He looked at the activity around him and realized they were preparing to load him into a waiting ambulance. He had no idea how long he'd been out but it had to have been at least fifteen minutes or so.

"Well, this is embarrassing."

She smiled a little, then winced; the movement must have pulled at her swollen face. "You're going to be all right. They've managed to stop the bleeding for now, but they're likely going to have to operate to remove the bullet and repair the damage. They're taking you to a hospital in Salt Lake."

He wanted to lie here and just listen to that sexy proper voice for a few years but there was something important he had to remember. It came to him suddenly and he frowned. "What about the kids?"

"I've already rung Pam and given her the shortened version of what's happened. She's fine with the children staying there as long as you need."

"And you? How are you?"

She gave another of those lopsided smiles. "A few stitches and a little ice and I should be right as rain."

A paramedic stepped forward, a burly man with no hair and a handlebar mustache. "We need to load you up now."

"Do we have to? I hate hospitals," he muttered.

Jane laughed a little. "It's only a few days. I'm sure you'll muddle through."

A second paramedic and a couple of men he recognized as FBI agents moved up to load the stretcher into the back of the waiting ambulance.

"Wait a minute, please," Jane said.

She laid her cheek to his, then kissed him softly on the mouth. "Thank you, Mason, for what you did back there."

I love you. He thought the words, but the time didn't seem right to say them aloud, even if he could get his throat to work past the lump in it.

Later. He would tell her when she came to the hospital.

He eased back onto the stretcher and didn't even complain when the medics shoved the oxygen back on his face, his mind full of extremely pleasant images of Jane pulled to the side of his bed, holding his hand and reading to him in that delicious voice.

She didn't come to the hospital.

Twenty-four hours later, Mason was going crazy with worry. He thought maybe she'd gone back to the ranch for some much-needed rest but when Pam brought the children to see him earlier in the afternoon, she said she hadn't heard a word from Jane and hadn't been able to find out where she might be.

When they left a half hour later, even Charlie seemed more subdued than usual and Miriam just looked at him in disappointment because he hadn't kept his promise to bring Jane back to the Bittercreek.

He couldn't seem to get through to anyone who would tell him anything. Finally he managed to reach Cale's cell phone.

"Hey, how are you?" the agent said. "I called to check on you in the night and they said the surgery went well but you were still in recovery and couldn't talk. I've been meaning to call all day but things have been crazy around here today. With the files we found on Djami's laptop, we've cracked the VLF wide open. There are some mighty happy people in the crowd you used to hang with right about now."

"Where the hell is Jane?" Mason cut in.

A prolonged silence met his question, then Cale hissed out a curse. "You mean nobody told you?"

He could swear his heart stopped but the monitor beside his bed continued blipping. "Told me what?"

"I'm sorry, man. I should have thought to let you know. She's been in FBI custody since yesterday."

"In custody? What do you mean *in custody?*"

"We had no choice, Mason. You know that. The evidence against her was overwhelming. We couldn't just let her walk away."

"The evidence against her is complete bullshit!" He thought of his sweet Jane in jail, frightened and alone while he lounged around here, and had to fight the urge to toss the phone through the window.

"I know that and you know that. But we had to follow proper procedure to make sure. You'll be happy to know she's in the clear, though," Cale went on. "Our computer guys found nothing on Djami's laptop to link her to the plot or the group and one of the men you shot yesterday came clean and confessed he helped Djami plant the evidence against her to discredit her."

"So where is she now?"

"I don't know. We had no more reason to hold her so she was released."

"When?"

"About a half hour ago. I'm sorry. I thought she would have called you from the holding facility."

Why didn't she? he wondered, hurt and confused. Didn't she think he would want to know? And if she wasn't in FBI custody anymore, where had she gone?

He was damn well going to find out. He ended the call

to Cale and slid out of bed, ignoring the ache in his shoulder and the slight wooziness in his head from the pain meds they shoved into his IV.

Ten minutes later, he had managed to pull his jeans on one-handed but he realized he was going to need help with his shirt, starting with removing the IV.

He pushed the nurse call button, then sat on the bed to shove on his boots. He was still working at it, chagrined at the sweat beading on his upper lip, when he heard the quiet whoosh of the door opening.

"I'm done with this," he growled to the nurse without looking up. "I need you to take out this damn IV or I'll yank it out myself."

A startled silence met his demand and then his visitor spoke. "I can certainly try. But don't you think you'd rather have a nurse?"

That voice. That wonderful, sexy voice. He lifted his gaze and found Jane standing in the doorway, looking small and delicate in a dark-blue business suit. Her eyes were shadowed and her face still swollen and bruised, but she was the most beautiful sight he'd ever seen.

He felt like his world was finally right again.

She was blushing, he realized, and he wondered why until he realized she was staring at his still-bare chest.

She cleared her throat and lifted her gaze to his. "Um, where are you off to in such a hurry?"

"Looking for you."

Jane barely heard him, too fascinated by all those rippling muscles. Good heavens. When she finally registered his words, she could only stare at him.

"Looking for me? Why?"

"Maybe because I had no idea where the hell you were.

Why didn't you tell me they were detaining you? Didn't you think I'd wonder why you didn't show up here at the hospital?"

"I didn't want to worry you. You had enough to deal with here and you needed your strength to recover from your injury. There was nothing you could have done to expedite matters, anyway."

She had to admit, even knowing he couldn't have changed things, she would have dearly loved to have him with her during her ordeal in FBI custody.

It was a nightmare she never wanted to repeat—the long hours of questioning, the utter exhaustion, trying to keep things straight in her mind when all she wanted to do was rush to Mason's side and make sure he was all right.

"I was worried about you."

His voice was low, intense, and she felt her last ounce of strength trickle away. The long night of worry and strain finally caught up with her.

"I've been such a bother to you. I'm so sorry." To her dismay, she started to cry and couldn't seem to stop.

Mason stood and crossed the room, then pulled her into his arms, bare chest, sling and all. She settled against him, careful of his injured shoulder.

"You have been a trial," he said. "I haven't been shot over too many women before."

She made a sound that was half sob, half laugh. "You're not making me feel better!"

"That's funny." He grinned suddenly and the sight took her breath away. "I'm suddenly feeling a hell of a lot better."

She had no idea what to say to that so she just decided to enjoy the moment, soaking in his heat and his strength.

"You should have let me know what was going on. I've

been out of my head wondering why you didn't call or come by or anything."

She sniffled one last time then pulled away just long enough to grab a tissue from the box on his bedside table.

"I had to do this myself, Mason," she said after she'd wiped her eyes. "For once, I had to handle things on my own to prove that I could."

She gave him a shaky smile. "I believe I've finally convinced anyone who would listen that I'm not a terrorist."

"I'm sure that's a relief."

He leaned forward and she held her breath, certain he was going to kiss her, but before he could the door opened and a round, cheerful-looking nurse in flowered surgical scrubs came into the room.

"You buzzed, I think. Sorry it took me a moment to get to you. We had a crisis down the hall. Is everything okay?"

Mason stepped away from Jane and she shivered. "I'm ready to get out of here. Can you take the IV out?"

"Tired of us already, are you? Your orders say maybe tomorrow so I'm afraid I'm going to have to talk to the doctor about that, Mr. Keller. Why don't I check your vitals while I'm here and then I'll go call your doctor and get back to you?"

Mason looked vaguely embarrassed. "Do you have to?"

"That's what they tell me."

While she hooked up a blood pressure cuff, Jane retreated to the armchair in the room, wondering if she ought to leave.

"Everything looks good," the nurse said after a moment. "Your heart rate's a little accelerated but that's all. You haven't been doing jumping jacks in here, have you?"

"No," Mason said.

Jane wondered at his abrupt tone, until she remembered what they'd been about to do when the nurse came in. He'd been about to kiss her—could that have raised his heart rate? She had to admit, she found the idea intriguing.

The nurse punched the stats into the computer by his bedside, then walked out of the room with a promise to come back after she'd talked to the doctor. She left a slightly awkward silence in her wake.

"So what are your plans now that you're a free woman?" Mason asked after the nurse left.

Jane looked down at her hands, already dreading the future. "I'm not sure. I suppose I'll go back to London and… and try to put all this behind me."

He said nothing for so long that she finally lifted her gaze to his. She found him watching her closely, an odd expression in his eyes that made her insides flutter.

"Or you could stay."

She stared at him, unsure what to say.

"I know two children who will be very unhappy to see you leave," he said, then paused. "And so will I."

She swallowed, her heart pounding so loudly she was certain he must hear it. "Mason—"

"I understand that your life is there, but I don't want you to go."

She shook her head. "I don't have a life in London. Not really. A few friends, a flat I don't particularly care for, a job I can live without. I realized since my memory returned yesterday that I've been hiding out from life. I don't take any risks, I don't try anything new. I go to work, I come home and that's about the extent of it."

"So you won't be missing much if you come back to the Bittercreek with me."

She curled her hands together, stunned that he would ask after all she had put him through. She wanted to—oh, how she wanted to—but at the same time, she had come to a sad realization while she'd been in that holding cell.

"You don't even know me, Mason. Those days at your ranch, that wasn't the real me. With the amnesia, I could be anyone I wanted. I could be brave and clever and exciting. But Jane Withington is not any of those things. Since Colombia and my father's death, I'm afraid of everything. I'm shy, I'm boring and I'm a terrible coward. What if you don't like that person very much once you get to know me?"

He was silent for so long she thought he must have seen the wisdom of her words.

She should leave now, she thought. Go and nurse her broken heart somewhere private. Before she could make her legs cooperate, he was there in front of her. He pulled her to her feet, clasping both of her hands in his uninjured one.

"I know all I need to know. I know you're wonderfully kind to two hurting children. I know you're brave enough to fight for what's important—you saved my life, Jane. Did you think I didn't see you going after Djami with that *jagpang* so he wouldn't finish me off?"

He paused and when he spoke, his voice was gruff. "And, most important, I know I love you and if you returned to England, you would take my heart with you."

She let out a stunned breath, but before she could respond, he kissed her. His mouth was warm and sweet and the emotion in his kiss brought more tears to her eyes.

After far too short a time, he pulled away slightly. To her amazement, this incredible, strong man who raced into a room full of vicious terrorists without a thought to his own safety now seemed hesitant, almost uncertain of himself.

"When Djami's FBI agents were taking you away from the ranch yesterday, you said you couldn't love a man who had nothing inside him but suspicion and mistrust."

"I was hurting and frightened, Mason. I shouldn't have said that."

"No, you were right. I spent so long walking through ugliness and filth that I couldn't recognize someone good and wonderful when she walked into my life. I should have trusted you. My heart did from the first but my head took a while to catch up."

Joy burst through her like a vast field of flowers opening to the sun. She smiled, wondering what Harry would say. "Better late then never, Agent Keller," she said with a smile.

He kissed her again. "I love you, Jane," he said against her mouth.

"And I have been in love with you since I was fifteen years old and you first came to my rescue."

Something else had been ratting around in her mind all night and she wondered if he would think her crazy if she said it. No, she was done with being timid.

"Don't you find it odd that our paths would cross again after all these years?"

He kissed the corner of her mouth and she shivered. "I don't know," he murmured. "I haven't really thought of it."

"I have. And you know what I think? I think something led me to you, to exactly that mountain road you would be traveling on."

She thought of the way those lorry doors had broken free at just that point in the journey. "I think someone knew I would need you and put me right where you couldn't help but stumble over me."

"Well, if that's true, I owe whoever it was a cigar. Finding you was the luckiest day of my life."

Mine, too, she thought.

Thank you, Harry.

Though it was probably her imagination, she thought she felt just the lightest touch of lips on the top of her head, and then it was gone.

* * * * *

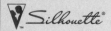

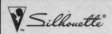

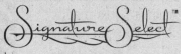

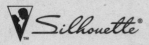

COMING NEXT MONTH

#1383 LIVING ON THE EDGE—Susan Mallery
Bodyguard Tanner Keane expected his assignment to rescue a
kidnapped heiress to be a no-brainer. And yet Madison Hilliard
wasn't at all what he expected. As passion sparked between them,
it was clear that his offer to keep her safe was anything
but. Would their combustible attraction stand in the way of
bringing down a deadly enemy?

#1384 PERFECT ASSASSIN—Wendy Rosnau
Spy Games
Her father was an assassin and after his murder, Prisca Reznik
took on a target list of her own for revenge. On her mission, she
encountered the very sexy Special Agent Jacy "Moon" Maddox,
who was responsible for her father's capture. Could the man she
meant to kill be the only man who could save her?

#1385 HARD CASE COWBOY—Nina Bruhns
No one ran faster from love than ranch foreman Redhawk Jackson,
until Rhiannon O'Bronach, his benefactor's niece, arrived and
made working together a necessity—and a sweet torture he'd
never envisioned. As they ran the ranch and dealt with its
hardships, Redhawk began to wonder if this tough-as-nails
woman was a threat to his future…or the key to his happiness.

#1386 WHISPERS AND LIES—Diane Pershing
Investigative journalist Will Jamison was sniffing out a story
that led him to an old friend. But little did he know the mystery
of veterinarian Louise "Lou" McAndrews's past would draw
him closer to her in every way. Not only had he stumbled upon
a secret that involved a powerful politician, but Lou's strength and
beauty made him rethink his vow to remain unattached. Could he
love her and keep her out of harm's way?

SIMCNM0805